~ The Lincolr

Lindum Scribes will donate £1.00 from the sale of this book to Childline Lincolnshire

Childline, essentially a child's 999 service, is very much a local, regional and national service, catering for specific local needs whilst serving children across the country.

Childline was launched in 1986 by Esther Rantzen on BBC's "That's Life". In 1994, **Childline Lincolnshire** came into being – with a dedicated free phone number specially for Lincolnshire Children (0800 389 5272). This made it easier for callers to be connected to the dedicated service for the County. Initially, Childline Lincolnshire was able to operate six hours a day, seven days a week. From April 2004 however, due to the unforeseen withdrawal of some major funding, this service can now only operate for four hours a day. Unless more money is raised, this will undoubtedly be cut again and would be a substantial reduction in the service. The impact on the children in Lincolnshire is worrying.

All money raised by Childline Lincolnshire goes directly to fund the specially designated Lincolnshire Lines.

~ The Lincolnshire Tales ~

Published in the United Kingdom of Great Britain and Northern Ireland by

Lindum Scribes
22, Tudor Road
Lincoln
LN6 3LL
Website address: www.lindumscribes.org

Edited by Stephen Wade and Colin Johnson

Typeset by Duet Marketing

Printed and bound in the United Kingdom by
TJ International
Trecerus Industrial Estate
Padstow,
Cornwall
PL28 8RW

Email address : www.tjinternational.ltd.uk

~ **The Lincolnshire Tales** ~

14 writers have contributed a total of 25 stories, on a variety of themes, but all with a common link to the county

School Run ~ A Knight Forgotten

One Link in a Chain	by **Peter Warwick**	4
The Lawnmower ~Mike and Helen	by **Colin Johnson**	30
Recipe for Love	by **Sally Smith**	43

Just Hanging About

Wait For Me Always	by **Anita Yorke**	56

Come Here Often

Early Morning Callers ~ The Picnic	by **Katy Holderness**	71
The Great Lincolnshire Challenge	by **Paul Stafford**	90
If only the Window Had Opened?	by **Marjory Grierson**	110
Jump for Freedom ~ Fatal Love	by **Julia Peach**	120

To Have and To Hold

Workplace Experiences	by **Elizabeth Selby**	137
Roman Steps ~ Search for a Model	by **Sharon Horne**	143
A Diary of Dates	by **Jay Michaels**	154
The Mirror ~ The Courier	by **Lisa Spinner**	172

SCM Ghost Hunter Ltd

The Top Prize	by **Mavis Wilkinson**	179
Bad Satellite Rising	by **R.G.**	187

School Run   by   Peter Warwick

As she waved goodbye to her daughter at the school gate, Cathy could not help herself. Her head was turned inexorably to face up the road, to see if it was there. Of course it was, as she knew it would be. The dark blue Ford was parked in its normal position, about thirty metres from the gates. A gentle pulsating flow of exhaust indicated that the engine was silently ticking over. The tinted glass hid the occupant, but Cathy could detect the gentle red glow of a cigarette, and yet the windows were all firmly closed.

Cathy felt a stab of ice in her heart. It was happening again. Yet who would believe her? Anxiously she turned back to wave farewell to Becky. She was not there! She felt a sob well in her throat, and the beginnings of a panic attack. She turned to look down the road. An empty space occupied the spot where the Ford had been parked. She turned back to the playground, a hoarse cry escaping her lips

" Becky!"

" She went inside with one of the teachers". One of the other mums, Lorna, was stood at her side, a wry smile on her face. "They soon forget you, don't they? Are you all right? You look a bit pale".

Cathy nodded weakly, and even managed a halfhearted smile. But she knew that she was not all right. Things had not been all right since Estelle Simpson had disappeared, supposedly enticed into a stranger's car, six months ago, and since then, the police had not uncovered a single trace of her. It was as though she had never existed, that the slightly out of focus photograph that had dominated newspapers, shop doorways and house front windows for weeks, was of some smiling illusion pulled from the pages of a book of fiction. Cathy had viewed the anguished parents, appearing in the harsh spotlight of the media, wide-eyed and bewildered, and wondered how she would cope if her Becky were snatched. It was an unending nightmare, made all the worse as Estelle had been a classmate of Becky's.

The passing of the months had not helped. Other parents, as concerned as Cathy initially, had now lapsed into a sense of apathy that comes with the march of time. They still talked occasionally, in their little groups huddled at the school gates whilst waiting for their children. Hushed whispers, at how Louise Simpson had aged, why, she had completely let herself go, and had no interest in her other children. Life had to go on, didn't it? Cathy witnessed the sniffs of the self-righteous, and the smug grins as their charges came out from school intact.

But Cathy knew the school was being watched, that the perpetrator was already planning his next action. But whom could she tell?

She decided, that day, to take her concerns to the police. After her visit, she questioned herself as to why she had bothered. The sergeant on the desk had been over polite, condescending almost.

"Yes, madam. Of course we understand your concerns, and let me assure you that our investigations are proceeding. We never give up on missing children cases. We'll check the car out for you, but I can assure you that you are most probably worrying needlessly." He smiled in his professional, reassuring manner. "It could be the father of the missing child. We know Mister Simpson has paid visits to the school on occasions. Acts as a sort of therapy for him."

Cathy had felt instantly guilty and selfish at the policeman's information. Of course, George Simpson, that poor man, and all the time she only had concerns for her own child. How did he feel? She had never met George, but the news reports of him portrayed a dark haired man, with pinched gaunt features, as he sat silently besides his distraught wife.

The next morning and the Ford was in its usual place. Once Becky was safely inside the school, Cathy strode determinedly up to the car, not really sure why, only that she knew she had to make some communication with Estelle's father.

She tapped on the darkened window, and could detect the outline of the man sat behind the wheel. He had shifted round to stare at her, but made no effort to lower the window. Cathy was confused. Why was he acting as if he wanted no contact with her? She was about to knock again, when, with a sudden roar, the vehicle shot forward, and disappeared swiftly round the corner. Cathy was numb with shock, and felt a cold stabbing of fear. She knew that the driver was definitely not Estelle's father. What had he to hide? Why wouldn't he face her? Her first instincts were to return to the police, but she could not face the condescending smile of the police sergeant again. She knew that her husband, Norman, thought she over reacted to every incident, and she no longer had the energy to confide in him. She was on her own, and she would have to remain extra vigilant.

It was two days later, when she found an unexpected ally. Louise Simpson.

Cathy had almost bumped into her when leaving the library after her usual Tuesday visit. Cathy loved books, any book, and could not get enough of them. The weekly visit was her one luxury, and never missed. It was with great surprise than she almost collided with the dishevelled figure of Louise Simpson. The poor woman looked tired, unkempt, and Cathy felt an overwhelming sympathy for her. After hurried, self-conscious small talk, Cathy suggested they go to the Copper Kettle for a coffee. Louise agreed. Within a few minutes, Cathy was wondering whether she had made an enormous mistake. What could they talk about? It could only be Estelle, their only connection, they had only ever crossed paths at school related functions. To Cathy's surprise, Louise was quite open about the issue.

"She's dead, you know. The police believe it, my husband believes it, and so do I. The trouble is, you can't admit it publicly, not even to your family. You would be called a coward, and not doing poor Estelle justice. I suppose that it is possible that she is alive somewhere. But I know, I *know*."

Cathy was taken aback as she uttered those words with such forcefulness, but none the less Cathy and Louise arranged to meet next day for coffee, and after a week, it was part of the daily routine. The talk centred less and less on the missing Estelle, and more on Cathy's family, and Becky in particular. Cathy put that down to Louise trying to get her thoughts back on some sort of normal theme, directing them away from the black cloud that threatened to engulf her. Louise had even taken to meeting Cathy at the school gates on a couple of occasions when she met Becky. They had ignored the questioning looks of the other mothers. Some had gone out of their way to avoid having to talk to Louise, as if she carried some disease that would contaminate their own lives and whisk their own loved ones away from them.

It was only after a week, that Cathy noticed for the first time that the Ford was no longer sat outside the school during start and finish times.

Over the next two weeks, Louise seemed to be always present, and Cathy began to question whether she had been too hasty in befriending her. She liked Louise, but she was so intense and opinionated, and Cathy realised, with a shock, that she had even started to dictate to Becky things she should be doing, and which television programmes she should watch. She had given her some of Estelle's favourite cuddly toys. That had amazed Cathy. How could she give away things that were intrinsically linked to her own daughter? Then, after three days constant wheedling, Cathy gave in to Louise's wish that Becky could have a sleep over at her house. She had crouched down before Becky, crushing her in a hug, and promising her that they would have the most fantastic time together. Cathy was now having serious doubts about her new friend's state of mind, and was determined that this would be the one and only time she could have her for a sleep over. She could not sleep that night, and Norman had gone and slept in the spare room. Guilt washed over her the next morning as a radiant Becky was delivered to the front door at the agreed time.

"Mum, we had a great time. Mrs Simpson let me play with Estelle's dolls and things. She has so much." Becky had turned and given Louise a hug. "Thanks so much."

Subtle investigation during the rest of the day revealed that her daughter had had tea, watched television, and then slept in Estelle's bed. George Simpson seemed to have been absent as there was no mention of him. Cathy felt a slight chill wash over her. Poor Estelle was missing, probably dead. It did not seem proper for Becky to be sleeping in her bed. Cathy made a decision. That was definitely the last time Becky could sleep over. She knew she had made the right decision next day when she met Louise for their usual coffee.

Louise had sat nursing her coffee, her faced relaxed and smiling. It was the happiest Cathy had seen her. Her next words chilled her.

"It was so lovely having Estelle back home last night"

"What… what did you say?"

Louise simply smiled, and took another sip from her mug. Cathy realised that she had not realised her slip, or her questioning. Louise was a woman re-born, relaxed, and happy, the faded washed out look she had worn had evaporated, and she was taking care of her appearance again, hair neat and fashionable, make-up perfect, dressed to kill. So what was Cathy so worried about? Surely it could not be wrong to help someone who was sunk in so much despair?

"Louise. Becky. It was Becky you had sleep over last night, not Estelle. Please, I don't think it was such a good idea, so I won't let her stay again. You are getting confused, you're not ready yet to have another little girl round the house. It's not fair for either of you!"

Cathy was shocked at the response from Louise. She slammed her mug down onto the table, ignoring the coffee that stained the white tablecloth and the startled glances from neighbouring tables.

"What are you telling me? You're trying to ruin the little bit of happiness I have." Her face turned ugly, white with anger as she half rose from her chair.

"Well, let me tell you, you won't take away what I have. It happened before, but I won't let it happen again! You're so smug and happy, but you don't want to share that happiness. Well, you're wrong, you'll see!"

"Louise…!"

Cathy was already talking to Louise's departing back, as she pushed her chair back sharply and strode out of the coffee shop.

Cathy sat for twenty minutes, clenching her hands, and hugging herself until the shakes had subsided. Louise had scared her. The woman was clearly unstable, and she had let her own daughter spend the night with her. With a sob, she realised the time. Becky! It was almost time for her to leave school. Weeping, she hurried the couple of hundred yards to the school gates, unaware of the questioning looks she was receiving from those she passed.

She was just in time. Most of the children and their mothers were already leaving, with just a small clutch of children and parents talking by the gate. With relief, she spotted Becky, her darling Becky, peering, as yet unconcerned. Cathy grabbed her roughly, encompassing her in the strongest of hugs.

"Mum, what's up? Are you ok?"

Cathy realised she was creating attention, and forced herself to calm down. She smiled weakly, and pushed Becky back at arm distance.

"Course I am. Just worried as I'm a bit late."

It was two days later when Louise rang Cathy.

"Meet you at eleven, at the Copper Kettle, ok?"

A surprised Cathy had murmured assent, wishing she was strong enough to resist. Louise was sat waiting for her at their usual table, smiling broadly as Cathy entered. She acted as if nothing had occurred, complimenting Cathy on her outfit, and how much she had been looking forward to sharing a coffee with her best friend. Cathy felt her spirits sink. It was all so unreal, yet she felt herself being inexorably drawn ever tighter into Louise's grip.

"I'm going for a ride up to Maiden's Head tomorrow, I think Becky would love to come. The views are absolutely wonderful."

Maiden's Head was the name given to a rocky promontory just outside of town. Legend had it that shipwreckers' wives would stand there, waving lanterns to lure ships onto the rocks on dark turbulent nights. Even today, on a clear sunny day, it was only too easy to imagine stricken vessels dashed to pieces on those sharp, black rocks forty feet below. Cathy shuddered inwardly.

"No, I'm sorry, but… I've got to take Becky to the dentist tomorrow, just for a check up, you understand."

Louise's face wrinkled her disappointment, and then cleared as if the problem had been solved. For one fleeting moment, Cathy thought she detected a look of cunning on Louise's face, and then chided herself for being paranoid.

"Well, no matter. Perhaps another time. Estelle loves going up there, especially when the seas are rough."

Cathy knew she had to break away from Louise's influence, to find a way without upsetting her. The episode in the Copper Kettle was all too vivid in her mind. Becky had been asking when she could go for another sleep-over, and Cathy had answered as vaguely as she could. Becky did not need to know just yet that there would be no more sleep-overs.

The next day was Thursday, dark and grey. It was late November, and the shops were already crammed with premature Christmas offerings. Cathy had a deep depression weighing down on her, something was wrong; she had felt uneasy all day. Now, she scurried her way past the shoppers, anxious to meet Becky. She was late again, delayed by the tardy arrival of a plumber who had come to fix a leaking radiator. The usual gaggle of mums and children were wending their way from the school gates.

"Hi, Cathy." It was Lorna. "I'm surprised to see you here."

Cathy felt the coldness envelop her. Hardly daring to ask the question, her voice was little more than a croak.

"What do you mean?"

"Well, your Becky. She's already left. She was…"

Cathy sobbed and turned back to the road, not hearing Lorna anymore. There! The blue Ford was there, and even as she saw it, its engine revved. Fear and desperation had supplemented all reason in Cathy. With a scream of anguish she threw herself in front of the car, bouncing off the bonnet to land on her back in the road. Ignoring the pain in her back, which would plague her for months to come; Cathy leapt to her feet, and reached for the driver's door, yanking it open. An astonished face peered up at her. She momentarily glimpsed the features of a young man with short hair, casually dressed in jeans and bomber jacket, and beneath a white tee shirt, suddenly spattered with the blood from his shattered nose as Cathy swung a fist into his face. She ignored the white hot pain of shattered knuckles as she looked beyond the driver, seeking her daughter. The car was empty, but she became aware of the sharp staccato and crackle of radios as someone asked Alpha Charlie what the hell was going on, and why was he not in pursuit.

Cathy was confused. What was going on? Where was her daughter? She was suddenly aware of people around her, of the flashing blue light of a police car and a friendly arm round her shoulder. Dazed, she was guided to the patrol car, and sat down heavily in the rear seat. She was aware of another man as he sat beside her.

"Mrs Parker, I'm Detective Inspector Jarvis. This has been an awful shock to you I know, but the delicate nature of our investigations meant we had to keep you in the dark."

"What investigations? Where's my Becky? What is going on?"

The police man leant forward, and held her arm gently. "The disappearance of Estelle Simpson. I cannot tell you too much, only to say that the Simpsons have been under observation. Unfortunately, we had not allowed for this afternoon's events."

Detective Inspector Jarvis spoke softly but firmly.

"Your daughter was collected by Louise Simpson. Please, don't worry; it will be only a matter of time before we pick her up. The plan was for my detective to follow her, but at this moment he is in no fit state. Talking of which, we had better get your hand looked at!"

"No, it's alright. Please, let's get Becky back. Why aren't you looking for her?"

"We are, Mrs Parker. Mrs Simpson is driving a red Fiat. Every policeman in the area is looking for that car."

"Maidens Head! That's where she's gone. She had already asked me if she could take Becky, and I said no. Oh please. I think Louise Simpson is unstable, there's no saying what she will do."

The policeman leant forward and issued instructions to the uniformed officers in front. Messages were relayed by radio, and then they were off, sirens blazing through the gathering gloom and past the curious.

Within minutes they came to a halt at the gravel track that led to the viewing point at Maidens Head. The first thing Cathy saw was the dark outline of Louise Simpson's Fiat, parked at the very cliff edge. Cathy followed the detective out of the car, but he held her back from making a mad dash to the car.

"No, we must be patient, and try to talk with her."

"But Becky…"

Even as she spoke, they both heard the engine of the Fiat roar into life. Its lights cut through the gloom, illuminating the long grass on the cliff edge that bowed before the wind. The wheels spun and the car leapt forward, disappearing into the darkness. The crashing of the waves below hid any sound as the small car embedded itself onto the rocks beneath.

With a moan, Cathy sank to her knees, as despair and grief washed over her. She was dimly aware of shouts and torches flashing as she was helped back to the car.
She sat there unaware of time or events that unfolded around her. Becky, her Becky, that was all she could think of. In those few brief moments her daughters short life played through her mind like a film clip, from the moment she had held her at birth, the laughs and tears, and above all, the love she felt for her. Life without Becky was un-imaginable.

"Mum! Oh Mum!" Her mind was playing tricks on her, she knew that, then she was jolted into reality as small arms enfolded her and hot tears wet her face as the figure of her daughter burrowed into her like a small animal seeking refuge. Then they were both laughing and crying at the same time, mother and daughter welded as one.

During the following week, Detective Inspector Jarvis explained what had happened, and with the delicate interrogation of Becky, the missing pieces were added to complete the investigation.

George Simpson had been the chief suspect from almost day one of the investigation. Louise had covered for him as best she could, but police investigations had revealed a man who harboured an intense and un-natural jealousy of anyone who diverted his wife's attentions away from him, including his own daughter. That he had killed her, the police had little doubt, but the location of Estelle's body was a mystery. When Louise had turned her love to Becky, George Simpson simply redirected his jealousy. He dominated Louise completely, and the police concluded that he had ordered her to collect Becky from school that day. This she had done, and then in a rare act of defiance, had grabbed Becky and ran once they were at Maidens Head. The arrival of the police had convinced George Simpson that things had run their course, so he had simply driven his car over the cliff. His body was recovered next morning. Police had found Becky shivering in the long grass, but of Louise Simpson there was no sign.

Cathy had nearly forgotten the events of those dark November days. Christmas had come and gone, and they were well into the New Year. The future beckoned brightly. Until one day, Becky mentioned she had been looking out of the classroom window one morning, and spied Louise stood by the gate. She had vanished by the time the school had finished…

A Knight Forgotten   by   Peter Warwick

The wind moaned and tugged remorselessly at his parka as he stood between the twin rusted rails of steel that divided the forlorn platforms either side. Jimmy Burton ignored the elements, and savoured the moment. Everyone has their own favourite image, that one heart stopping location that wants to make them linger and soak up the moment as long as possible. For some, it is a tropical sunset framed by palms in silhouette, for others, the grandeur of snow-capped mountain peaks reflecting the sun, or the village church in springtime, fronted by masses of daffodils. Jimmy's just happens to be railway stations. Or, to be more specific, abandoned, run down, deserted and decaying railway stations.

What is it about old stations that captured him so? Perhaps it was the ghosts that lingered, those countless souls who once crowded these now deserted platforms, the remnants of countless tearful farewells and home-comings, forgotten emotions still clinging to the cracked masonry and peeling wood that once gazed proudly down on those majestic giants of the steam age, as they hissed, bellowed, and thundered about their business.

Bagley was like so many other stations he had visited, but still with its own unique atmosphere. It crouched here, abandoned, on the edge of farm land, once an important life line for the community, but now left to rot away, forgotten by a thankless world. The station had served the local sugar beet processing plant, bringing in workers from all over the county, and countless freight trucks piled high with beet. Half a dozen times a day, the great engines wheezed and rumbled their way over the flat farmland with their cargoes, like faithful reliable beasts of burden, never complaining, always there to serve their masters.

Then, suddenly it was all over. The beet processing factory was declared redundant, a change of policy, and within six months it was closed down. The railway staggered on for a few months, suddenly utilised to take equipment away from Bagley, then the work dried up, and then the announcement was made. Bagley would close down; the line could not make a profit. So that was that. Within weeks the station adopted that run down abandoned look that swiftly overtakes any building left un-used. The rails lost their shiny veneer, and soon became coated in a film of reddish brown. Weeds sprouted, and the goods yard became home to adventurous wildlife. Within a year, the nearby beet factory was demolished, the land returned to farming, and the station was left in the hands of the elements.

Now, forty three years later, Bagley station was little more than an empty shell, a deadened husk in place of a once vibrant and alive cluster of buildings. Windows stared across windswept farmland, the shattered glass like sightless eyes as the wind moaned and groaned through open doors and leaking roofs. The waiting room was now bare, only the blackened fireplace testament to its previous occupation, along with a barely legible remnant of a summertime timetable still clinging to a graffiti adorned wall. The ticket office window was still intact, and a close look through the grime smeared glass revealed an upturned high backed chair, the sole remnant of busier days.

Jimmy Burton climbed up on to the platform, and stood, as though awaiting some long overdue train, and savoured the moment. His head was thrown back, face into the wind, eyes closed, and a half smile on his lips.

Ah, yes! This was what he lived for, and this part of his visit was only the first act.

At least, that was what he was praying for. He just hoped that the farmer who had rung him up earlier the previous day had got his facts right.

Jimmy Burton was the owner /editor of a small circulation magazine entitled 'Days of Steam'. He was a railway fanatic, and knew without doubt that, had the days of steam continued, he would have been a driver. Both his father and grandfather had been drivers, and he had grown up in a home that always smelt of coal dust and steam, of walls adorned with monochrome pictures of railway men, smiles enhanced by blackened features as they posed proudly against the monster driving wheels of their charges. But Jimmy was denied his birthright. Diesel and electrification put paid to that, so he channelled his energies down different paths, writing for enthusiasts' magazines, joining societies and clubs and spending his weekends restoring now derelict tracks and rolling stock across the country. After a few years freelancing, Jimmy took the plunge and published his own magazine. Now, three years later, *Days of Steam* was a steady seller, and had built up a reputation as a factual and accurate publication amongst the highly demanding and critical enthusiasts who populated the Steam world.

Yet Jimmy was not satisfied. There was a black hole inside which no amount of volunteer work and writing could fill. A magazine was all very well, but what Jimmy craved was his own engine. An impossible dream.

Until that phone call.

"Is that Mr Burton?"

"Yes, it is. How can I help you?"

"Are you the Mr Burton that owns the railway magazine?"

"Yes. Who are you, and how can I help?"

The line was crackly, and the caller sounded unsure, as if unused to talking to strangers on the telephone. Jimmy decided that he had a rural accent, and his next words confirmed that.

"My name is John Evans, and I run a farm down here near Bagley. I was wondering if you would have the time to get across to visit me in the near future. I think I have something that might interest you."

That had been two days ago, and Jimmy had travelled to Bagley as soon as he could. Interested? That was an understatement. Now, he glanced at his watch. Five past two. Evans had said he would meet him at the station at two. Where was he? Or was this all a hoax?

"Mr Burton? Sorry I'm a bit late."

John Evans was nothing like Jimmy had imagined him to be. He was a small wiry man, dark haired and scrawny featured, his jacket unopened, disdainful of the wind that tugged at them both.

They exchanged pleasantries, for all the world just like two business men meeting on any railway station, apparently unaware that they were surrounded by crumbling decay. Evans gestured for Jimmy to follow him, and jumped easily down onto the track, setting off without waiting to see if his guest was following. Jimmy smiled inwardly. A bit of an odd bod, of that there was no doubt, but friendly enough. A few yards outside of the station boundary, and the rail track abruptly ceased. What remained was a well worn dirt track, elevated above the neighbouring flat farmland, the embankment snaking outward and across as far as Jimmy could see. It was an outstanding feat of engineering just to have built this embankment, let alone lay a track.

"We've about a mile to walk. At least it's not raining."

Jimmy smiled and nodded, and the rest of the walk was in silence. Jimmy was glad, as it gave him chance to put what Evans had told him on the phone into perspective, now that he was actually here.

Evans had told him how the railway had run across their farmland, from Bagley station and on to the coast. It was a single track line, used mainly for freight, but there were also passenger services operating about three runs each day. About a mile from Bagley, a small length of spur track veered off to a maintenance shed, which was hidden behind a screen of oak trees and runaway blackberry bushes. Here was where the routine maintenance and repairs had been carried out. This spur line was owned by the Evans family, who were paid a yearly rent by the railway. When the line was closed down, the track from the station to the coast was ripped up and sold for scrap. The spur line was left intact.

"So you see," Evans had said, "the railway just up and left us with about three hundred yards of track and maintenance shed, and they never bothered returning."

Jimmy was excited.

"That's great. I'll have to come down and see what you have in there. Any old rail tools and equipment are of enormous interest, you could most probably make a fair bit of money at auction!"

"Rail tools and equipment be damned. They left behind a whole bloody engine!"

How Jimmy had contained his excitement he never would know. Evans could not answer his many questions on engine type, number of drive wheels etc, only that it was:

"Big and rusty, but still in one piece!"

They came to a Y, the leg veering to the left suddenly consisting of rusted track and rotting sleepers. Jimmy's heart was racing as they rounded a gentle curve and into a copse. Nestled down under the trees, as though sheltering from the elements, stood a wooden maintenance shed. The track vanished through padlocked doors and into the shed.

"I keep it locked. Don't want no prying eyes. As I told you on the phone, I only had my first look inside a few days ago. Been locked up all these years, Dad kept a load of old trailers and suchlike in front. The old bugger knew what was inside, just didn't want to let on! Never even told me. Now he's gone, and I thought it was about time I sorted a few things out. Never expected to find what I did!"

"Get on with it!" Jimmy wanted to shout, but managed to keep quiet.

Evans strode up to the wooden doors, and fumbled for what seemed an age, until he withdrew
the lock and chains.

Together, they pushed the creaking doors apart on rusted runners, and only when they were completely open did Jimmy stand back and rest his eyes on the treasure inside.

"Oh my God!" he whispered. It could not be, yet it was.

"It's an Urie/Maunsell Standard Arthur!"

Jimmy was quivering with excitement. Slowly, he stepped towards the great beast, and reached out tentatively to touch its cold metal, running his hand gently lest he should waken it from its lengthy slumber.

"How did you escape the scrap yard?"

He slowly walked round the locomotive, withdrawing a battered reference book from his parka pocket as he did so. He noted the number on the front, 30804. A quick check confirmed what he suspected and now he knew the great machine's designated name.

Sir Cador of Cornwall. Supposedly scrapped in 1962. Yet how was she here?

Mesmerised, Jimmy continued his survey. Her great driving wheels were taller than a man at six foot seven inches, her length more than sixty two feet, and she weighed more than seventy six tons. Built in 1926, this magnificent specimen had escaped the fate of its siblings by hiding out here for more than forty years. There was only one surviving example according to the record books. Sir Lamiel was shown proudly up in York. The great engines were originally designed for freight, but different versions were developed, resulting in the Class 5 as a passenger express. It was considered romantic at the time to name them after King Arthur's knights, and the public and enthusiasts alike loved them in that last nostalgic age of steam. So, the question remained. How did Sir Cador end up here?

"Worth the trip down here, do you think?"

Evans' voice on his shoulder startled him from his thoughts.

"I couldn't tell you how much, Mr Evans. This is fantastic. I don't think you realise how valuable a find this is. I'm just bewildered as to how she ended up here."

"Well, the only person who might know is George Murcott. He was here at the time, working with Dad. He might be able to shed some light."

So it was, an hour later, Jimmy and Evans found themselves in the Murcott's parlour. Now in his eighties, George was sprightly and voluble as his wife Nancy produced a pot of tea for her surprise guests. After Evans had made the introductions, Jimmy could barely contain himself as he fired questions at George. George took his time, as though relishing in the moment, taking an age to produce his pipe and meticulously pack it with tobacco, then lighting it with a well practised flourish. He gazed at Jimmy through the smoke, a merry glint in his eye.

"Well, young feller, I can see you are excited about old Bess over there, so perhaps I'd better put you out of your misery." George told his story.

When the beet factory was shut down, freight trains were in and out of Bagley all the time, utilised to take away equipment and anything of any value. There was a deadline, as they were told that the salvage contractors were due to start soon on taking up the track. The rush led to a shortage of suitable engines available, and Sir Cador, or Bess, as George called her, had been drafted in to help. She was at the end of her working life and due for scrap, but the authorities had thought she was good enough for one last task. Unfortunately they were wrong, as Bess gave up the ghost on the second day she was there. A severe loss of working pressure the engineer had told him, and what did the railway expect from a 36 year old veteran? She had been ignominiously shunted onto the Evans spur line whilst other engines continued the work. And there she sat, even as the salvagers moved in and tore up the track.

Evans senior had watched with amusement as both railway men and salvagers disappeared, and no one had even commented on the great locomotive stood under the trees. A week later and Evans senior and George had hooked a tractor to Bess, and slowly eased her back into the maintenance shed. Evans closed the doors on the locomotive, and had given George a wink.

"Mum's the word now George. We'll let things die down for a bit, then see what she'll fetch for scrap."

But of course, they never did. She sat there undisturbed until now.

Jimmy's wildest prayers had been answered; he had his own engine. Well, technically, she still belonged to the railways, but he knew they would be only too pleased to hand her over to someone who wanted to restore her. He knew he had some convincing to do, but he would put it to John Evans that this would be a solid business proposal, that enthusiasts from all over the country would flock to see Bess, and that money would be forthcoming. Sir Cador would be the centre piece of a museum, sponsored by Jimmy's magazine, and run by the enthusiasts who read it.

There was one other incentive, which Jimmy was keeping silent about. At least for now.

Before leaving the locomotive, Jimmy had jumped up into the cab for a quick look. Everything was intact, even down to an engineer's rag draped carelessly over a lever, and long dead ashes in the firebox. An old enamel mug, left on a ledge, still bore the blackened fingerprints of its owner. But, most exciting of all had been Bess's log book, tucked away by the driver's window.

Inside, neatly written in large, deliberate letters was the name of Sir Cador of Cornwall's last driver. Joseph Burton. Jimmy's father.

One Link in a Chain   by   Peter Warwick

It had been there all the time, shut off from the outside world by a solid curtain of overgrown apple trees, and knee high grass. Stephen had eased himself through the dense barrier, ignoring the clutching branches that tugged at his clothing, and the angry buzzing of disturbed wasps that rose from the crushed rotting fruit beneath his feet.

There it stood, sad and decayed, the neglected remains of great Aunt Irene's summerhouse. Empty window frames stared at him accusingly, and the remnants of a door hung crazily from one hinge. Stephen had seen the photographs of happier days: Irene and Claude, sat in front of the summerhouse, surrounded by laughing children and friends, eating from laden picnic tables as attentive servants hovered in the background.

His feet sank through rotten wood as he crossed the decking, and reached the dark interior, where he waited for his eyes to adjust to the gloom. The roof looked remarkably sound, and, knowing where to look, he turned his attentions to the left corner, in the gap between roof and wall. He ignored the pungent smells of rotting wood and animal droppings, as his eager fingers searched the small space, giving a small cry of triumph as he grasped something cold and damp.

He withdrew a small tubular leather case, the sort that would carry a small telescope. The once shiny leather was now dull and covered in mildew. Stephen rapidly withdrew, back into the gardens, and into the bright sun.

With shaking hands, he pulled off the end cap, and tilted the container on its end, and viewed its contents with excitement.

It was only in the few recent years that Stephen had learnt of Irene's existence, but it had only taken one visit for him to become totally enamoured with the grand old lady. Aunt Irene exuded an air of faded gentility, a relic from an age where liveried servants served diners with pre-dinner drinks, and the men retired to the smoking room after eating. All that was gone now, and Irene had lived alone in the great house, visited only by her cleaner who visited three days a week, fetching her shopping for her at the same time.

Irene appeared to have no friends, living in self imposed isolation, and when Stephen had enquired as to why she distanced herself from the townsfolk, she had replied:

"Oh, my dear boy, I'm afraid that it's the other way round. They have no wish to be seen with me!"

Irene had turned to look out across the once grand gardens, now sadly reduced to overgrown lawns and abandoned fruit trees. A delicate lace handkerchief appeared as she dabbed at glistening eyes. She stood, and gestured for Stephen to follow her onto the patio where two ancient chairs awaited. Here, the air was warm, redolent with the smells of the French countryside that Stephen had grown to love.

Irene had sighed. "I'll try to tell you what happened, Stephen. It needs telling, painful though it is."

Spring 1944, and activity had increased dramatically in recent weeks. Claude had been killed in the early months of the war, and Irene regarded it her duty to play her part in the defeat of the Germans.

Irene had been recruited by British Intelligence in what they described as a low risk position. She would run a letterbox, like hundreds of others across occupied Europe. She would leave messages for an unseen contact to collect, messages she collected herself hidden in her groceries which she picked up daily from the patisserie. The messages were coded, so it seemed harmless to enemy eyes if uncovered.

The summerhouse was Irene's post-box. The leather case from an old telescope belonging to Claude was perfect, fitting perfectly into its hideaway against the roof. Her innocuous notes were picked up regularly, and Irene had accidentally witnessed her contact one afternoon, ducking back into the shade of apple trees lest she was seen herself. She recognised Henri, a swarthy, muscular farmworker from the outskirts of the village now risking everything to help liberate his country.

Despite being English, Irene had attracted surprisingly little attention from the small German garrison in the village. An officer had visited once, his punctilious manner at odds with his commiserations concerning her dead husband.

Now there were rumours sweeping the area of an imminent allied invasion, and the countryside seemed to be teeming with more German troops. Irene's mailbox was in almost daily use.

Irene was awoken early one morning in mid May by loud hammering on her door and guttural shouting. A black clad officer, accompanied by two soldiers carrying automatic weapons greeted her. He bowed slightly, and then informed Irene in perfect French that she would accompany him immediately.

They drove only a short distance, to a farm which Irene recognised with a sinking heart as the one at which

Henri worked. She was led into a barn, and gasped once her eyes had adjusted to the gloom. There, lined up against the rough wooden walls, were six men. Badly beaten and shirtless, Irene recognised Henri almost immediately. For one second their eyes met, and then Henri dropped his gaze. In that short moment Irene was horrified to see accusation.

"Madame Chermoinaux, you may be wondering why I have brought you here at such an early hour. I believe these men are working for the resistance. So far, they have declined to talk, but I am sure they will in due course! Meanwhile, I am interested in their chain of command, who gives them their instructions." He reached forward suddenly, and grabbed her face tightly, forcing her head back.

"You, Madam, are English, so you will forgive me for viewing you with suspicion. Now, I ask you, do you know any of these men?"

Fear constricted her throat, and for one shameful moment she thought she had wet herself. She could only shake her head.

For what seemed an eternity his cold eyes locked onto hers, and then with a grunt of frustration he pushed her away.

"I hope for your sake that you are not lying, Madame."

The next days passed in a haze of fear and sleeplessness. She wanted desperately to go to the summerhouse to retrieve the message she had left for Henri, telling him to abandon that night's mission. It was then, with horror, that she realised that she could not remember leaving it there. There had been so many messages, and on the day in question she had been called away to visit a sick friend. Had she betrayed Henri by not leaving him the message that could have saved him and his friends? Irene simply did not know.

It was on the third morning and the same officer came for her. Irene was convinced this day was her last, and looked back tearfully as she was driven away, for one last glimpse of the home she had shared so happily with Claude. The officer obviously had his suspicions about her, else why this attention?

Dazed, she exited the car, and with a sinking heart she realised why she had been collected. Henri and his friends stood against the church wall, facing a troop of soldiers, rifles shouldered carelessly. The officer strode up before them, then turned and addressed the villagers. He told them they were about to witness the fate of all collaborators, that this was a warning. The next moments were a blur, shouted orders, the snick and click of readied weapons, and the sudden deafening crash and the wails of the townsfolk. Irene had walked back to her house, her mind full of visions of crumpled bloodied bodies, and mindful, even then, that the people she had known for years seemed determined to avoid her. They had witnessed her arrival with the officer and made their own conclusions. She was tainted.

Irene's resistance days were over, and she never went near the summerhouse again. During the heady days of liberation she was thankful to escape with merely having her head shaved; things could have been worse if it had not been for the intervention of an English officer. Even when she was identified as working for the resistance, hardened objectors insisted she was a double agent.

So Irene had spent the following decades living on her own, not wishing to leave the house she had shared with her beloved Claude.

On receiving news of her death, Stephen had come to help settle her affairs, as she had no relatives apart from him. He had read the letter she had left him, and the closing paragraph had stuck in his mind.

"Stephen, throughout these years I have asked myself repeatedly if I had left a letter for Henri to abort the mission. I dared not look, so I have died a coward. Please check for me, perhaps it is still there. If so, say a small prayer for my soul."

Now, Stephen looked down at the faded letter in his hands.

"Mon plus cher. Nous ne pouvons pas nous revnir ce soir! Soyez en contact. F."*

Stephen knew the F stood for Francois, her code name. For sixty years that message had sat here waiting to vindicate her, yet fear and guilt had kept her away.

Tears filled his eyes, as Stephen made his way from the house to the village church.

Aunt Irene could rest in peace now.

* My dearest one. We cannot meet tonight! Will be in touch. F.

The Lawnmower   by   Colin Johnson

For Sale : Qualcast Electric Lawnmower, excellent condition, new blades, recently serviced £50 o.n.o.

I put the advert in the Echo, our local newspaper a couple of weeks after George was buried. I thought it only right to leave some sort of interval, as a sign of respect, if you know what I mean. It was the first time I'd ever put an advert in a paper, but the smart young man behind the counter at the newspaper office was very helpful and he let me have two extra words free, nice of him. I thought you'd have to fill out a form for an advert, but they do it all on computers these days. Everything seems to be computers now don't you think? It made me laugh when they talked about the millennium bug, do you remember that? As if it was the end of the world because it would mess up the computers. How did they think we got on before computers?

It was the first time I'd been into town for quite a while really. I never have a chance to get out of the house much, what with the cleaning, washing, and ironing. Then there's cooking George's dinner for him, so it'll be ready for when he gets home from work, it keeps you busy, so I don't really have much time for going out during the day, at all.

I like to keep the house "nice" in case of visitors. I polish and hoover right through the house everyday, and then I'll do what I call one of my special jobs, like washing the paintwork or dusting the pelmets or cleaning the inside of the windows. I don't have to do the outsides as the window cleaner does those once a month.

I first met George at a dance, not like one of these discos that they have now. A proper dance, with a band on the stage playing Glenn Miller tunes, proper music that you could dance to. He looked very dapper back then, with his neatly parted hair, slicked down with brylcream, and his perfectly pressed trousers and black polished shoes. Very smart, not scruffy, like some of the boys back then. Some of them, they looked like they'd been dragged through a hedge backwards. Not George. He asked me to dance, very politely, and I was taken with him straight away. He had a good job, a white collar job as we used to call them, in the accounts department, at a local office.

"A job with prospects," he said.

The following week, he asked me to go out with him, to the pictures. I was really excited, looked forward to it all week. The night we were going out, he came to call at my house, so that my parents could give him the "once over", and he was bang on time, to the second. As the parlour clock struck seven, the doorbell rang, and there he was on the doorstep, as bright as a new penny.

We were courting for about six months when he popped the question, and I said yes straight away. Couldn't wait to be married, settle down as they called it, have a family. I couldn't wait.

We didn't have a big wedding, nothing flash. Just family and a few close friends at St John's , then a sit down meal, round the corner in the back-room of the social club. Mum got a bit squiffy, and then she started sobbing because I was leaving home. No foreign honeymoons in those days. It was back to work on the Monday for both of us. Me, down at Klingers, the cleaners in the high street, and him in his office. We needed the money you see, cos we were saving up for a deposit.

We've always lived in this house, since we bought it the year after we were married. It was beautiful when we first moved in; all of the houses in the area were new then, with tree lined roads and lots of small roundabouts. George is most particular about decorating, and always likes to get his paintwork just right. Everything's got to be rubbed down, have an undercoat, and then have two good coats of topcoat, to keep the weather out. White, we always have white on the outside, with a dark blue front door.

On the inside, we prefer brilliant white on the paintwork and doors, and tasteful wallpaper, nothing too bright or fancy. We like everything to match, co-ordinated they call it now. Wallpaper, curtains, cushion covers and table cloths – flowers, we particularly like patterns with flowers.

My mother was in awe of the kitchen when she first saw it. "All mod cons", it was advertised as, and there they were. A cooker, which lit itself when you pressed a button, a fridge, with a freezer compartment, for ice trays, like you see in those Doris Day films, and, most impressive of all, a twin tub washing machine.

Although we'd talked about starting a family, we never did have any children. Not long after we moved in, my sister Vera came over one Sunday with her two little'uns. Typical children they were, tearing about everywhere, tracking dirt in from the garden, toys all over the living room, noisy, screeching at the tops of their voices, and enjoying every minute of it, but George didn't. After they'd gone he kept talking about what a mess they'd made, and how he couldn't live with that everyday. All talk of starting a family stopped after that.

I suppose it was being tidy and organised that made George so successful in accountancy. "A place for everything, and everything in it's place," he used to say.
Not long after we'd moved in, he'd labelled the inside of each kitchen cupboard with the contents. Tins in one, packets in another, plates stacked neatly in a third, and glasses, in descending height order in a fourth.

In the summer, we always go to Chapel St. Leonards, for the middle two weeks of July. George always maintained that this was the best time to go, as it was cheaper then, because it was just before the school holidays start, but the weather was still decent. We always stay at our favourite bed and breakfast; with Mrs Reynolds, on the front. She's such a charming lady, and we've come to feel that room number nine, which we stay in, is our home away from home.

It's a lovely town, always wins the best kept town award, and the municipal gardens are a treat. Each day, we get up at eight, George has the full English breakfast, with extra toast, whilst he reads the paper. Last year, there was a bit of a to do, as Mr Reynolds had changed the station on the radio in the breakfast room from Radio Four, to a music station, but, George soon had it changed back. "Thirty years I've listened to the *Today* programme in the morning, and I don't intend to stop now", he said.

After breakfast, we stroll around the shops for a bit, and then along the seafront until lunchtime. There's a lovely little café near the bandstand, where we have a pot of tea, and a bite of lunch, and then we take out a couple of deckchairs in the afternoon. George has a favourite spot, on the seafront, so we always sit there until the sun goes down and it gets a bit chilly, when we go back to the b & b.

We always do, oh sorry 'did', the shopping at weekends, as we can go in the car to that big Tesco's on the by-pass. We've had the same car for these last ten years now, Japaneese it is. Very reliable, and very economical. George used to check the fuel consumption by recording the mileage for every journey and comparing it against the petrol receipts, then, he'd list it all on a chart, which hangs on the wall in the study. We used to shop at Tesco's in the High Street, every Saturday morning, from ten till twelve, and then we'd go into the Hare and Hounds for lunch, and two drinks. So, it was a bit of a shock when they said that it was closing down, as people preferred to go to the new store because it was bigger.

When we first went there, we were amazed. Such a big shop – so clean and bright and tidy, and so many things to choose from, I've never seen so many different types of biscuits in one place. Not that it really matters to us, as we always have digestives. They're George's favourites digestives are, so that's what we have. After a while, we found a very nice pub nearby, who also did a very good Steak and Kidney pudding (George's favourite), which he said was just like the one at the Hare and Hounds.

A creature of habit was our George. Always worked in the same office these thirty – five years. Always left for work in the morning at the same time, and came home at the same time, on the dot. They offered him a promotion the other year, but he turned it down, 'cos he'd have had to work in a different department, and he didn't fancy the change. He likes his desk and chair, says "it gives him a sense of stability, in an ever changing world." Every morning, I'd make him a flask of tea, and give him a small Tupperware container with four digestives. He'd have two with a cup of tea for elevenses and two with a cup of tea at four o'clock "teatime". Every day. Same thing really with our dinners; Monday/cold meat from Sunday, Tuesday/rissoles, Wednesday/sausages, Thursday/ meat pie , Friday/fried fish and chips – every week. Thirty-five years of the same meals, every week.

That was how I got started on the evening classes. I mean, there's not a lot of planning or preparation time goes into cold meat, now is there, and as Monday night was George's lodge night, and there's never very much on the television, I thought it would be a bit of a break. I did start off with the embroidery class, as I'd told George, and I was well on the way to making a shaker style New England quilt cover, but somehow, there seemd such little point. We never have any visitors, and after dinner George always falls asleep in front of the television, so no one would see it except me.

Then one week, I stopped to look at the notice board as I came in and discovered a course in home electrics. It sounded really interesting, so I joined.......and it was really interesting. Wiring plugs, ring mains, insulation, running spurs, I was fascinated. It was a whole new world......without George.

On week four, Mr Maynard, our instructor, explained all about safety. He showed us how easy it was to turn even the most humble of household items into death-traps, "if you weren't careful with your wiring". Then he explained about electrocution and especially about the dangers of water, and how important rubber soled shoes were.

George loved gardening. He'd be out in all weathers, rain or fine. Weeding his flower beds, tending to his roses, trimming his hedge until he'd got the angles just right, mowing his lawn to get those lines he so loved. He always wore his green wellies, and he was most upset when he couldn't find them the other week. He had to wear what he called "unsuitable footwear", which let the rain in and made his feet damp.

It was the coroner who said "how unlucky" George had been. "A victim of circumstance. Not many people can have a lawnmower that long with faulty wiring and have it go undetected", he said, and to be mowing the lawn on a wet day, without rubber soled shoes was just asking for trouble. Would you like another cup of tea ?

Or another biscuit maybe? I've got chocolate hob-nobs!

Mike and Helen   by   Colin Johnson

Mike :

You keep asking me the same questions and I keep giving you the same answers, so I don't know why you want me to go over it – "Just one more time". Maybe, you think I'm gonna say something different. Maybe, you think I'm gonna let something slip. Some secret bit of information that I'm holding onto. A clue – something to "help you with your enquires". Who knows!

Well, here goes then. One more time, for good luck.

I've been going out with Helen for exactly six months. I first saw her in Starbucks, the one in the centre of town, not the one they've just opened on the retail park. It was a Monday, one fifteen, on a glorious hot summers day in June. I'd walked up through the High Street, and I'd had to stop as usual when a train crossed it at the level crossing. What a daft idea that is, a railway line that runs straight across the High Street, and people get paid a fortune for town planning. Anyway, I came in through the door of Starbucks, and there she was, sitting in one of those comfy armchairs they have, smiling and talking to Maggie, her friend from work. Both of them had Mocha Frapachinos, and those heated up rolls, paninis? I think that's what they're called. Maggie had a piece of cake, I'm not sure what sort, and Helen had her favourite, a blueberry muffin.

The first thing I noticed about her, was her eyes. Blue they were, bright and clear, just like on the telly when they show you the sea in Greece or Turkey on those travel programmes. She was wearing a blue blouse, and it matched her eyes, and a tight black skirt , with smart polished black shoes. As you may have noticed, her hair is blonde, straw coloured. She wears it long, and with her tanned skin, she looks like a film star. I just couldn't take my eyes off her.

I spoke to Maggie first, when Helen had popped to the loo. When she returned, we were deep in conversation, and it just carried on with Helen included. We hit it off straight away. She was so easy to talk to. Don't get me wrong, I don't normally chat to strange women, I'm not that sort of chap, but this just sort of happened so naturally, and I ended up leaving Starbucks with them, and walking back to the shop where they both worked.

Lunch at Starbucks became a regular thing. Mondays, Wednesdays and Fridays. The three of us. When the weather became autumnal, they switched from frapachinos to hot drinks. Helen had a white chocolate mocha and Maggie had Hot Chocolate – both with cream. Personally, I always stayed with the daily blend, just as nice and a fraction of the price. On the other two days of the week, Helen would work through lunch. She'd often be on the service counter, which gave us a chance for a chat, on our own. Don't think I've got anything against Maggie, I haven't, but she's always hanging around, always there, never leaves Helen's side for a second. So it was nice to talk to Helen alone, if you can count a busy shop as being alone.

The first time we went out together on what I'd call a proper date, was Friday 9th September. We went to the cinema on Brayford Wharf, to see the new Tom Hanks film. I hadn't had a preference, so I left it to the girls. They chose the film, and I went along with it. Well you do when you're first going out, don't you. Actually, I really enjoyed it. We all bought ice creams, and the seats were great. A romantic comedy they called it on the posters.

Afterwards, we had a drink in one of the bars alongside the river, trendy place, smoked glass, discreet lighting, overpriced if you ask me, and, no decent bitter on draught. As it was a nice night, they had tables and chairs outside, and you could watch the swans gliding up and down.

After that, we settled into a regular routine. Lunch, the cinema, a bar – not always the same one. Sometimes, we went up to the Cathedral area, where there are a couple of nice pubs, sometimes, the other way, down the High Street. Just prior to Christmas, the shop started to get busier and the girls had to work through lunch more often, but Helen and I still found time to be together, and I was starting to think it might be time to meet her parents, or bring her round to meet my mum. I felt sure they'd get on like a house on fire.

I'd started to feel that what I had with Helen was something special, that she was someone special. Girls talk about Mr Right, to me, she was Miss Right, or maybe even Mrs Right.

This evening, or I suppose it was last night, now that it's getting light, I'd planned to take her somewhere special, just the two of us. I'd booked a table at the new Italian in the High Street, the one with candles on the tables. I figured it was romantic as Tom Hanks and his girlfriend had been in one similar to it in the film we'd seen. Cinemas and Bars are alright but you can't talk properly in either, and I had something important to talk about, us, our future together.

So, I waited for Helen outside the staff exit to the shop. She usually comes out about 20 minutes after closing. She didn't see me as she came out 'cos I was standing off to one side. Then, suddenly, this young bloke, wearing a dark jacket and scarf, a college type, came straight towards her from the opposite side of the road and grabbed her. He was holding her really tightly so she couldn't move.

Well, I couldn't let him manhandle her like that so I leapt forward and pulled him off her. He squared up to me, his eyes blazing with anger, and then he started for me, so, I hit him with the first thing that came to hand, my motorbike helmet.

All I wanted to do was to get him away from her. I could hear Helen screaming at him. I didn't mean to hit him so hard. I caught him on the side of the head and he went down like a sack of potatoes, holding his head in his hands. Then, from out of nowhere, you blokes arrived. How is she? Is she alright? When can I see her?

****

Helen:

How is he? Is he alright? When can I see him? I'm sorry, I'm sorry, I'll calm down, it's just that it's all been such a shock, a nightmare really, and I'm not sure if I've woken up yet.

Start at the beginning. O.k. then. I first met him about six or seven months ago. Maggie, my best friend introduced us. We seemed to hit it off straight away. He's easy to talk to, kind, makes me laugh, and he's the best looking man I've ever been out with. All my friends are jealous, especially Maggie. She keeps reminding me how she knew him first.

I don't have to describe him because you've seen him yourselves, but people say we make the perfect couple, and, although we haven't known each other very long at all really, I think we're going to be together for a long time, maybe, forever.

For my birthday, he bought me a necklace and earrings, beautiful they are, I wear them whenever we go out. I would have been wearing them tonight, if I'd had a chance to go home and get changed. We were going out to dinner, it was a surprise, somewhere special he said.

Then, at Christmas, he bought me this watch. Lovely isn't it. Must have cost him the earth. We both live in Lincoln, although at opposite ends of the City. He lives to the South, towards Newark, and I live with my parents in the North. When he came in to see me at BHS where I work, the other day, he was talking a lot about summer holidays, so maybe, it was that he was going to talk about tonight. Oh I do hope he's o.k.

Tonight…yes, sorry, tonight. Well, we finished sorting out the sales stock after the store closed and generally tidying up. As I knew he'd be waiting for me, I was really keen to get away quickly. I pulled my coat on in a bit of a rush and shot out of the door. I didn't see him at first, it was all a bit of a blur. I was swept off my feet, as he grabbed me, and kissed me……then that madman attacked us!

Oh! I do hope he's alright, that nutter really hit him hard with his helmet. I saw the gash on Dave's head, he was in such pain. Oh I do so hope he's alright.

You see, I told you I was being stalked, right from the very start. Maggie was the first one to notice him. Motorbike leathers, filthy hair, and those horrible black rimmed glasses. His acne, and his bad breath, it made me feel sick just to see him and he seemed to be everywhere. If we went to Starbucks at lunchtime, he was there. We stopped going in the end, but he just hung around the shop. Maggie tried to stay around, so that I didn't have to deal with him on my own, but she couldn't be there all the time.

I knew he wasn't right in the head when I had to serve him one day, and he muttered something about my eyes being the same colour as my blouse. I mean, good grief, I was wearing a BHS overall!

Then, he started turning up in the evenings as well. Once a week, Maggie and I go to the cinema, a girl's night out. He must have been hanging about, watching me for ages. Maybe he was following me home from the shop, watching my house from across the road. Ugh! It makes my skin crawl just to think about it.

Anyway, Maggie and I went to see the new Tom Hanks film, and like a bad penny, there he is, bold as brass. We buy ice cream, he buys ice cream. We buy tickets for the Tom Hanks film, he buys a ticket for the Tom Hanks film. Worst thing is, he's sitting right next to us. That's the problem these days, you buy a ticket and you have to sit in the seat you're allocated. Used to be, you bought a ticket, and you could sit anywhere.
He obviously asked for a seat next to ours and the guy serving thought we must be together.

After the film, we went to a nearby bar. Ten minutes later, he's there, staring at us. Creep. Every time Maggie and I go out, it didn't seem to matter where we went, there he was. We varied the night, we sometimes went up by the Cathedral, sometimes down the other end of town, and still, he was there. One night, Maggie completely lost her rag, went over and gave him a piece of her mind. Told him basically to "f-off" and do you know what he said? That she was "coming between us". Him and me, an "us", don't make me laugh.

I was at my wit's end. I just didn't know what to do, so Maggie suggested I come and talk to the police. Fat lot of good that did me. All you did was tell me he was "probably harmless", that he'd "lose interest" and that Dave was not to hang about and "sort him out" as that would be assault, and you'd lock Dave up.

When it carries on, I come to see you again, and by now, you obviously know who he is, and you start talking to me about care in the community. Care in the community? What about care for the community? What about caring for us, by treating people like him, so they don't stalk girls. What about that, eh?

Recipe for Love   by   Sally Smith

The romance had not been going particularly well, in fact Brad, the object of her desire, had not actually noticed her yet. Milly decided that she needed to take drastic action.

During her lunch break from the Cathedral gift shop, she hurried down Free School Lane toward the newly renovated Library. She hoped that three quarters of an hour would be enough to search the shelves. Her Brusha boots made the long walk up and down Steep Hill possible in less than ten minutes. Each boot contained the recycled remains of witches' redundant brooms within their soles. This gave them a remnant of lifting magic, and made them the lightest footwear of all time. Hikers bought them by the thousand, finding that they could trek for miles without tiring, and there was a huge market amongst teenagers who thought it was cool to hover over the dance floor.

Milly paused for a moment and looked at the impressive library building. She loved the way that the council had managed to retain the original 1914 façade despite all the rebuilds in the last two hundred years. Inside however, the library had been completely restocked and brought up to date with every conceivable publication. Milly thought that the solution to her problem with Brad might be amongst the centuries of knowledge.

She walked across to the desk in the reference section and felt in her pocket for her CrystID. Her fingers closed around the familiar short wand of clear crystal that stored all her identification. As fast as she could she waved it over the scanner, playing her usual game, trying to move too quickly for it to read who she was.

"Welcome, Milly," intoned a computerised voice and the turnstile glowed to let her know she could go through. She passed through the dimensional displacement shimmer and into the library.

Its vast expanse stretched before and above her, reaching as far as the eye could see and beyond. The Lincoln City planners had really hit upon a wonderful idea when they had discovered how to make buildings bigger on the inside than on the out. It had solved all the overcrowding problems in the city.

Having read about the concept of this magic in her weekly magazine, Milly really couldn't see why it hadn't been discovered before. The idea was so simple to anyone with a basic grasp of Dimensional Dowsing. All you needed to do was to use a couple of Birch twigs to dowse for an extra dimension, and then build inside it.

Now, however, she was not thinking about the technicalities of dimensional building. She looked around, unsure where to start her research. Usually she could reach the high shelves of fiction quite easily with her Brusha boots. Even older people wore them in the mile high library. However, Milly needed to research some very tricky ideas, so she looked around for a FLiCa, Flying Librarian – Carpet, to guide her. She saw two of the hovering FliCa's begin to undulate toward her when they saw her gazing uncertainly at the aisles. The leading one was a dingy green Paisley pattern.

"Oh no," she knew that, despite her determination, she would be far too embarrassed to explain her problem to a dull old doormat.

To her relief, the FLiCa was suddenly distracted by the antics of two wizards. They were noisily stocking the Mobile Library Portal. The carpet oscillated admonishingly, at which they rudely and magically removed the noise from the air, and stacked the books even higher. The wobbly tower of Mills and Boons and large print westerns tumbled down with a silent crash, and engulfed the FLiCa in a cloud of dust.

Muffling her laughter, Milly was thankful to see the other FliCa stopping in front of her with its colours flashing brightly. It lowered an edge, forming a step so that she could easily climb aboard. It gave slightly under her foot but was firm enough to support her weight. Gingerly she walked to the middle and stood with her arms out for balance. She was unused to the motion, and needed to concentrate on staying upright. The FliCa remained in a hover a few centimetres off the ground. Confused, Milly looked down, then realised that she had forgotten to say what she wanted. 'Er, Love Spells,' she said, 'A friend asked me to look them up.'

The FliCa moved. Surprised, Milly lurched backward but was deftly caught by a fold of the carpet, which then formed a perfect seat. Trying to recover her composure, she smoothed down her ruffled skirt. The carpet banked for a corner and Milly squeaked with fear. 'Ooh no,' she moaned and squeezed her eyes shut as the swift movement of the FLiCa overwhelmed her.

"Is something wrong?"

Startled by the voice next to her, Milly's eyes opened wide as she glanced around. There was no one there. She shuddered, she was fairly sure that the dimension in which the library had been constructed did not have ghosts but there was something distinctly spooky about the disembodied words.

"Can I help you?" the same voice asked.

"Where are you?" Milly said.

"I knew this system wouldn't work," the voice sighed. "Look down."

Milly looked down. Far below her she could see two people hovering on their Brusha boots. Each was engrossed in a book. Tentatively she waved.

"No, not them," said the voice. "Here, on the FLiCa."

Milly peered closely at the softly pulsing wool pile. Suddenly she could see a faint hologram of a tiny man standing on the deep purple area of the carpet.

"Umm, if you could move onto a different colour, I might be able to see you better," she said.

"What?" He glanced down at himself. "Oh, right." Obligingly he hopped across to a yellow area. 'Is that better?'

"Much," said Milly.

She studied the little man closely. He was about six inches high and see-through with a faint blue tinge.

"What are you?"

"I am here to help you,"

For one crazy moment Milly thought he might be a miniature fairy godfather who would grant her dearest wishes. She chuckled at herself. Everyone knew there was no such thing as fairies although wishing for Brad's attention would be easier than finding a love spell.

"No, I mean, what are you?"

"I am HoLi,"

Milly raised an eyebrow. "Well I can see through you but there doesn't appear to be any holes."

"I knew that was a stupid name too." He groaned. "It stands for Holographic Librarian. I'm here to help guide you through the intricacies of the library. FliCa's can take you to places but I can help you decide where you want to go."

"Oh, umm," said Milly. She was embarrassed at the thought of asking him about the Love Spells. Inspiration struck.

"I need to cook a very special celebration meal."

The HoLi looked puzzled and glanced at the shelves next to the hovering carpet. The spines on each of the books displayed titles in a distinctly magical font. *Spells of the East, Magic for Beginners, More Simple Potions for the Uneasy.*

"I think I had better check this FLiCa in for an orientation and alignment overhaul," he muttered and vanished for a second. The FLiCa corrugated with indignation and Milly patted it apologetically.

The HoLi reappeared and moved onto the yellow area. "Right, let's find you those recipes." The disgruntled carpet set off with a jolt that threw Milly backward again. It flew with stomach lurching swiftness past books on every conceivable subject. "How many is this dinner for?" said the HoLi, unruffled by the erratic movements. She could see that he was standing a few millimetres above the pile.

"Er, just two," she said, feeling trapped.

"Oh ho, obviously someone very special. What sort of food does he like to eat?"

"Well," she paused. She had never actually spoken to Brad for long enough to find out. In fact if the truth were known, she had hardly talked with him at all except in her imagination.

"Italian," said the HoLi. "Everybody loves pasta."

The FLiCa stopped abruptly, its movements suggesting that it was still upset at the slight to its seeking capabilities.

"Here," said the HoLi waving a hand, "is the largest selection of cookery books in the world."

Milly looked at the titles in front of her. The brightly coloured spines danced before her eyes:

120 Recipes from the Man Who Cooks ; Sweet Treats in a Jiffy ; New Ideas from Granny's Old Dishes.

"Um, is there anything simple?"

The HoLi floated up a couple of shelves and pointed. "How about this? *Celebrate in Style with Ease.*"

Milly pulled down the book and opened the glossy pages. *Swede Mousse with a Sauce of Clams.* Ugh. *Jellied Rabbit,* oh the poor thing, she flipped a few more pages *Terrine de Canard.* " What's that?"

She shut the book and decisively put it back.

"No, something simpler." Her usual style of cooking was self-heating plate meals. When she had lived at home, Mother had tried to teach her how to use the old fashioned microwave but Milly had not been interested.

Eventually after the HoLi had found several ever simpler recipe books, and Milly had rejected each one, they ended up with two which she felt could be of use.

"*Really Simple Ways to Feed Your Loved Ones,*" read the HoLi, and "*Create a Celebration by Boiling Water.* Are you sure that this is the impression that you want to give?"

"Not really, but I would rather do something easy than risk messing up anything more complicated."

The HoLi pointed at yet another glossy book. "Look, try that one. It's one of my favourites and it is very straight forward."

Milly placed *Lincolnshire Italian Recipes* on top of the other two books without bothering to look at the contents. All she wanted to do now was to go home and plan the meal for Brad.

"Thank you for your help," she said politely.

"You're welcome," said the HoLi, staring at her. "Um, forgive me for being personal, but is that how you usually do your hair?"

Milly's hands flew up; one grasped the single blonde plait while the other brushed ineffectually at escaped strands of hair. She nodded.

"It's just that with your bone structure," gabbled the HoLi, "you would look stunning with it short."

Milly was bemused. She had never heard of a hologram giving fashion tips. He directed the FLiCa to a different section of the library.

"Look at these styles," he pointed to a photo where the model's hair was cut short around her face, leaving wisps of it feathered onto her cheeks.

"See how this one defines her cheek bones, and here," he turned the page, "see how her eyes are highlighted."

Milly looked at the pictures. Maybe this was the way to make Brad finally notice her. She added it to her collection of books, eager to go home and study them.

"Thank you so much," she said."I really must be off."

The HoLi smiled. "Let me know how the meal goes," he said with only a suggestion of a shudder.

It was a week later when a subdued Milly returned to the library. She waved her CrystID across the scanner and the turnstile glowed and greeted her. As she pushed at the bar, it added "Nice hair cut, by the way."

Milly barely looked at her image on the computer screen. She had been so proud of the new style, enjoying the silky feel when she ran her hands through her hair. She had loved the way that the colours changed from deep purple to pale pink and back again, in a gentle but mature wave of tones.

Brad had not even noticed. She had handed him the invitation to dinner and then had watched in breathless shock as he had crumpled it up without a second look.

Devastated, she had not had the heart to look at the recipes and had furiously shoved the books into a bag ready to return them as soon as possible. As she placed them onto the counter, the HoLi popped up. "Did the meal work then?" he asked nonchalantly.

"No." Milly was still angry, and only too ready to blame the little hologram. "And if it hadn't been for you, I would have found a spell and everything would have been fine." The HoLi looked puzzled. "But you asked for recipe books… Oh I see… I think."

Ignoring him, Milly continued. "He didn't even come to my house and he screwed up the invite, and I had bought a new dress and… Oh I feel such a fool." She scrubbed away a tear that was slipping slowly down her cheek.

"Please don't cry," he begged. "Look, come in here."

A hand closed round hers. Shocked out of her tears, Milly looked at the HoLi who was no longer a six-inch high hologram on the desk, but a real person with warm comforting hands. He led her through the dimensional displacement shimmer into an office. "But you're real."

He laughed gently. "Of course. You didn't think I was really six inches high and blue did you? I just sit in my office and my image is projected out there onto the FliCas as needed."

He pulled out a chair for her. "Let me make you a coffee and you can tell me about the meal that wasn't."

Milly was embarrassed. "Oh, I can't. It was bad enough when you were six inches high but… Oh I just can't."

He didn't seem to be listening to her excuses and she watched as his tall figure quickly produced coffee and biscuits, setting them on a desk in front of her. It felt comforting to be looked after. He sat down and pushed the plate of biscuits toward her, then leant back nursing a mug. "I like your hair. I thought it would suit you short, but I would never have thought of the colour. It makes you look really confident."

"Something needs to." Milly cradled her coffee mug in her hands, the warmth slowly penetrating her fingers. She had felt cold since Brad's rejection. As she remembered his sneering face, she cringed and her eyes filled with tears again.

Vaguely she heard a chair scraping across the floor, then a strong arm slipped round her shoulders and hugged her gently. At the show of sympathy, Milly sobbed and covered her face with one hand. She felt the mug pulled from her grasp and some tissues pushed firmly between her fingers. Then the warm embrace returned. Milly turned her face into his shoulder and cried with frustration and anger that all her plans for Brad had come to nothing.

As the frantic weeping slowed, she became conscious of the gentle rise and fall of the HoLi's chest. For a moment she kept her eyes shut, not wanting to leave the security of his arms. Slowly, sensible thoughts began creeping back into her mind and reluctantly she pushed herself away, wiping her eyes.

"He can't have been worth it."

Not trusting herself to speak yet, Milly shook her head. She swallowed then took a couple of deep breaths before croaking. 'Thank you.'

"It was nothing," the HoLi returned her coffee mug. "All part of the service. You should see some of the floods of tears I have to deal with when people can't get the book they want. Why do you think I have a box of tissues at hand?"

Milly giggled wetly and sipped her coffee. "What's your real name? I can't keep thinking of you as the HoLi, not now that I have soaked your shirt." He rubbed at the dark patch on the front of his blue shirt. "It'll dry."

He held out a hand. "My name is Hugh."

Milly jumped up and shook it. "Thank you for all your care, Hugh."

Their hands remained clasped and she looked up into his dark eyes. She watched as his cheeks blushed. Suddenly very conscious of her own breathing, Milly said. "No, you're not blue at all, are you?"

There was stillness for a moment. Reluctantly she began to move away. "I must go. I have to be back at work soon." Their fingers parted slowly. Hugh rubbed the back of his neck then asked, "What were you planning to do with the ingredients?"

Milly was puzzled. "What ingredients?"

"For the meal that you were going to cook." He rushed on, his face crimson again. "I could come round and cook them for you. That is if you would like me to."

"Well," Milly didn't know quite what to think. The ingredients for the meal had been the last things on her mind.

"No, of course not." Hugh turned away. "You hardly know me. It was a daft idea."
He picked up her bag and handed it to her. "Well I mustn't keep you."

Moments later a bemused Milly had passed back through the dimensional displacement shimmer into the main library.

A week later, Milly let herself into her mother's bungalow in Thorpe on the Hill.

"Anybody in?" she called.

"Hello love."

She flattened herself against the wall in the hallway as her indefatigable mother whizzed past her, planting a kiss on her cheek in passing.

"I'm just on my way to the village hall. It's library day. You can walk up with me, dear."

Once a week the Mobile Library Portal visited the village hall. It was the County Council's latest idea for reaching the farthest parts of rural Lincolnshire. Books could be quickly and cheaply transported even to the remote villages of Rothwell in the Wolds, and Holbeach St Matthews in the Fens.

For a while the librarians had even tried the innovative idea of transporting the Portal straight into the reader's home, although that hadn't lasted long. Last time it had called at Mother's little bungalow, she had knocked her tea over as it had 'ported in, and there had been sparks and damp books everywhere. Ruefully the librarians had agreed to revert to 'porting to the village hall. Mother much preferred that anyway. It was the highlight of her week, combining her love of reading with an excuse for a gossip with her friends.

She reappeared with a pile of library books and dropped them into Milly's arms.

"Find my hover and put those in it please." She disappeared into the bathroom.

Milly fetched the shopping hover bag from the cupboard and began putting the books into it one by one. A familiar title caught her eye. "*Lincolnshire Italian Recipes,*" she read.

It was the same glossy book that she had borrowed and neglected to look at. She flipped it open idly and looked at photos of the author and friends tucking into various dishes. Suddenly she stopped. At a table beneath a large tree was a familiar figure, raising his glass to the camera.

"Hugh," she exclaimed. A thought struck her and she reluctantly turned the book to look at the author's picture on the back cover. Smiling up at her was the HoLi from the library.

"Oh my goodness, he must have thought me a total idiot." Milly buried her face in her hands. "No wonder he shuddered at Celebrations with Boiling Water".

"Who, dear?" Milly's mother bustled back into the room wearing her coat. "Come on, or else we'll miss the library." She briskly bundled Milly out of the front door, locked it and hid the key in a little extra dimension by the door.

"No one will find it there," she said and set off up the road. Milly, pulling the shopping hover laden with books, panted along behind her.

A happy noisy crowd had gathered outside the hall waiting for the doors to open. Milly's mother was soon in the thick of it, greeting her neighbours as though she hadn't seen them for months. She could email her friends three or four times a day but still chat for hours when they met.

"Milly," her mother reappeared and grabbed her arm, "Come on, we've got a place saved at the front of the queue."

Milly followed dutifully, her mind still engrossed with Hugh. He was really good looking but she would be far too embarrassed to go back to the Central Library now.
"A chef with a published book," she groaned to herself as the doors opened and the excited women pushed their way inside.

"That's right dear, and we're going to be first to get his autograph," said her mother.

Milly stopped and stared. There seated at a table, with piles of books on each side of him, was the HoLi. He looked up at her and smiled with surprise and pleasure.

"Milly. I didn't know that you lived here. Nice of you to come and support me." Quickly he picked up one of the books and wrote inside it before handing it to her. "Here, take this as a gift from me."

She took the book with her mouth open, but was jostled and shoved to one side before she could say a word to him.

Pushing her way to a relatively quiet spot near the fire exit, she looked at the copy of *Lincolnshire Italian Recipes* and turned to the title page where he had written.

"Please meet me afterward. In hope, Hugh."

Milly closed the book and smiled. Perhaps there was a chance after all. Her mother struggled through the crowd to her, happily waving her own copy of the book.

"Now dear, are you staying to tea?"

Milly dropped a kiss on her mother's cheek.

"No thanks, Mother. I think a friend may be cooking for me."

Just Hanging About   by   Anita Yorke

There was not much work to be had in Newark, so I headed off towards Lincoln, where I'd heard, jobs were easier to come by. As soon as I had got there, I found myself a job working as a labourer in the fields, digging over the soil after the winter, ready for the new season's crops to be sown. Once the seeds had been sown, I had to look for other work. There were jobs in other places, mending things like fences and roofs, feeding cattle or looking after sheep, and I even worked at the ironmongers for a while. I was happy, there was enough money to be able to eat and enjoy a few beers, plenty of different jobs so I didn't get bored. Life was pretty good.

There were some good looking wenches in Lincoln, too. I found one especially nice girl called Mary, and I saw her most evenings. On Sundays, we used to walk hand in hand by the river, chatting and laughing. She was a jolly girl, she enjoyed company, and liked to sup a beer or two with me. It was all very pleasant, until the day she told me she was pregnant.

Mary's parents called for me to go to their house, to see what was to be done about the situation. They said I had to marry Mary, to avoid the scandal of her being with child, and only sixteen years old herself. Well, I told them I didn't want to marry Mary, and maybe if I moved away from the area, it would be alright. Her mother told me that was stupid, it wouldn't make the baby disappear, and the whole village would still be able to see Mary getting more and more pregnant, with no husband to support her.Her father gave me two options. Either I married Mary and looked after her and the baby, which would be the manly thing to do, or I could go to prison for the rest of my life for what I had done. The authorities did not look kindly on men who got children pregnant.

Well, I didn't have much choice, did I? I certainly didn't want to spend the rest of my life in jail, locked in a dark, dirty, damp cell, being beaten and starved. All my freedom taken away from me for the sake of a wench with child? No way. So I agreed to marry Mary. We were married at All Saint's Church, where I thought it best that I didn't mention that I already had a wife and child in Newark, and after the ceremony, we walked the fifteen or so miles to Saxilby where we were to live.

Although we were nearly at Saxilby, Mary had to sit down at the side of the track, because she felt tired. She said that she was tired carrying the extra weight around in her belly. I told her to get up and keep on walking. She was only half way through her pregnancy, it was going to get much heavier before the end. If she couldn't manage to walk a few miles now, what would she be like just before the baby was born? Was she going to sit around feeling sorry for herself? Who would do the cooking and cleaning if she was too tired to do it? What kind of wife was she? She sat and cried, said I was uncaring. I told her to pull herself together and stop behaving like a baby. She just cried all the more. So I walked off and left her there. I went home on my own.

After an hour Mary hadn't arrived, so I wondered what she was playing at. I walked back out of the village towards the place where I had left her. She was still there, but not crying any more. She was dead. Beaten to death with a wooden hedge stake.

Of course, I was arrested straight away, and accused of murdering Mary. I told the authorities that I hadn't done it, but they wouldn't believe me. Mary's parents said I'd killed her because I didn't want to marry her, and I was trying to get out of the marriage. Well, for goodness sake, I had agreed to marry Mary so that I wouldn't have to go to jail. I wasn't likely to go and kill her, knowing that I would go to jail, would I?

I kept on telling everybody I didn't kill my wife, but nobody believed me. They even brought in a witness at my trial, some farm worker who said he had seen me do it. He told the authorities that Mary and me had argued, and that I had picked up a wooden hedge stake and hit her with it. He said I kept on hitting her until she was dead. I don't remember any of this. I don't remember hitting Mary. And I don't remember any farm worker being nearby that day.

The authorities agreed that I had murdered Mary, and I was to hang for the crime. The hanging took place at the castle, where a huge crowd had come to watch. Before Mary's death nobody knew who I was. Now, suddenly, everybody wanted to see me being hanged. And afterwards, they all followed the cart with my body on it, all the way to where Mary had been killed. Here a gibbet was set up, and my body was put into it. So I was hanged twice in the same day, once at the castle where I was hanged until dead, and then again near Saxilby where I was gibbeted.

For months people used to walk over to the spot where my body hung, so that they could see me. I was a sort of tourist attraction. The landlord of the Sun Inn at Saxilby, the place where I used to have a drink or two, bought the stake which was used to kill Mary, and he hung it over the fireplace in the bar. Aren't folk weird? Over at the track, which was now called Tom Otter Lane after me, my flesh rotted off me and there was just my skeleton left in the gibbet. Birds made their nests in my skull, and they raised their chicks in my head. After a while less and less people made the journey to gawp at me.

On the first anniversary of Mary's death, I decided to revive interest in me. I had quite liked all the attention I had got earlier, when the murder was still fresh in everyone's minds. I tracked down the witness from my trial, the farm worker who told everyone I had killed Mary. I still say there had been no farm worker nearby that I could see. Maybe he was lurking in the hedgerow, watching Mary and me. Maybe he was a Peeping Tom, or some crazy person. I know I didn't kill Mary. Perhaps he was the one who did it? Perhaps he was a secret admirer of Mary, and because he couldn't have her, decided nobody could. Perhaps he was the murderer.

So as I said, I tracked him down. You can do all sorts of things as a ghost that you can't do when you're alive. In the middle of the night, I went to the Sun Inn and got the wooden stake from over the fireplace. I went to where the farm worker lived, and "persuaded" him out of his bed. He was absolutely terrified. I made him follow me to the spot where Mary had been killed. He was only wearing his nightshirt. And I left him there, holding onto the wooden stake. He was found there in the morning, just as I had left him, clutching the stake which was dripping with fresh blood. He couldn't explain to anyone how he had got there. Or why he was there. Or whose blood was on the stake. He was taken home, shaken and cold, and the stake was taken back to the pub.

Well, that got the crowds back to the gibbet for a few weeks, and brightened up my lonely existence. They were alternately fascinated and horrified by the sight of my rotting bones and the story of what I had done. Poor innocent Mary had been completely forgotten by everyone except her parents, and here was I, the guilty scoundrel, remembered by all and the topic of everyone's conversation around the county. The landlord of the Sun

Inn also did well out of my little game, as people filled his pub, wanting to see the famous wooden stake. So I did the same again the next year, fetching the stake from the pub, getting the farm worker out of his bed and leaving him shivering and scared by the hedgerow, clutching the stake with fresh blood on it. And again people came to visit the gibbet.

By the third anniversary, the local people were already prepared. They set up a vigil in the pub that night, so that they could watch the stake disappear. I had to wait until they had drunk themselves to sleep before I could take the stake. Nobody had bothered to set up a vigil at the farm worker's place, and so again I made him get out of his bed. It was such good fun, and so easy to do. In the morning, there was the farm worker sitting by the side of the track, where Mary had died, with the stake in his hand. Many people came back to peer at me in my cage, and to wonder why these events happened every year. Was it a message from the dead?

That was the last time I played to the crowd. The farm worker couldn't take it anymore, and he hung himself. Well, there's guilt if ever I saw it. You don't hang yourself if you are innocent, do you? Do you think all this changed the minds of the authorities, Mary's parents, or anyone else for that matter? No, it didn't.

The landlord of the pub sold up that year, and nobody knows what happened to the stake. Was it buried somewhere? Did he take it with him? The gibbet with my remains in it finally collapsed after more than forty years, and part of the gibbet was bought by Lord and Lady Snooty-Buggers at Doddington Hall. They've got it displayed in their house. How strange is that?

Well, I've told you my side of the story. It's up to you now. Was it me who murdered Mary? Or was it that Peeping Tom farm worker? What do you think?

Wait For Me Always   by   Anita Yorke

As Catherine walked along the leafy lane, she felt the ground tremble beneath her feet, and heard the distant rumbling. She quickened her pace. A truck lumbered past, the driver unable to see her in her dark skirt and cardigan, as she stood with her back against the hedgerow waiting for the lorry to pass. Then she jumped into the roadway again and hurried towards the crossroads. Turning right, the rumbling noise was much louder and the ground shook. Catherine ran the last few hundred yards to the edge of the airfield.

Looking into the darkness, she could see the giant shadowy figures of the Lancaster Bombers, and the ant-like people in comparison working underneath the aircraft. Yet another engine started up, making the sound so loud that Catherine needed to put her fingers in her ears. The smell of cordite, smoke and engine fuel filled her nose and throat. The ground beneath her was shaking violently.

The engine noise increased, so Catherine knew that the aircraft were about to taxi to the runway. She watched the huge, dark beasts slowly amble along the taxiways towards the far side of the airfield, where they would wait in turn for take off. As they moved away, the noise died down a little and Catherine was able to remove her fingers from her ears. The smell of the engines still hung in the air.

Minutes later the first of the Lancasters dragged its bomb-laden fusilage along the runway, struggling against the weight to get airborne. It skimmed over the boundary fence, past Catherine, and rose slowly, majestically into the night sky. The sound was deafening, the earth vibrated. Moments later a second Lancaster hurled itself into the air, followed by another, and another. There were more and more of them. Was there no end to the number of aircraft taking off? Where were they going? What was their target? Were they going to bomb Hitler's ammunitions factories, or would their target be a town somewhere in the heart of Germany? That would mean the needless destruction of houses, and innocent people being killed. Catherine shuddered at the thought.

She had no idea which aircraft her fiance was in as it was not possible to see the letters on the side of the planes. Catherine knew that her Tommy flew in one called S for Sugar. She called out to him, although she did not know whether he was airborne already, or still waiting for take-off.

"Please come home safely, Tommy. I love you."

As the last of the aircraft disappeared into the darkness, Catherine imagined she heard Tommy's voice.

"I love you, Catherine," it said. "Wait for me. Always."

The engine noise eventually disappeared and silence returned, the earth became still. Catherine heard Tommy's voice over and over again in her head. In all the time that she had been coming to this spot, knowing that her beloved was going on another dangerous night bombing raid, and wanting to wish him goodnight before she went to bed, she had never heard his voice before. Why had he spoken to her tonight? What did he mean – wait for me, always? He was going to come home safely in the morning, wasn't he? He always came home.

Catherine must have been standing at the end of the runway for some time, as she suddenly realised that she was shivering. She turned and hurried back home. Her worried parents called to her as she walked through the door, but Catherine did not respond. She went straight upstairs to her bedroom. Sitting on the edge of her bed, she stared through the window at the black sky. Tommy's voice echoed in her ears. The tears began to fall.

Tommy Blond was full of life, always laughing and joking. Whenever the crew were feeling worried, Tommy lifted their spirits. Nothing ever seemed to worry or frighten him. There were two Tommys in the crew, and in order to distinguish them from each other, he was called Tommy Blond as he had a cascade of unruly blond hair. The other Tommy was the captain, who sported a huge handle bar moustache. He was called Tommy Tache. Catherine had met the crew when they visited the village pub. Catherine was immediately attracted to Tommy Blond's bubbly character, his love of life. He had been attracted to Catherine when he heard her sing as she accompanied her friend on the piano.

The last three months had been a whirl of love, laughs and enjoyment. At the weekend, Tommy had approached Catherine's father and formally asked permission to marry his daughter. Catherine thought she could not be happier. Knowing that the War interfered with many relationships, Tommy and Catherine decided not to waste too much time before marrying. They were to be wed the following month. She was in a frenzy of organising her wedding dress, the bridesmaids, and the wedding cake. There was just so much to do to make the day perfect.

As Catherine stared through her tears into the night, she felt the dream slip away. She knew that something awful was going to happen. She knew that Tommy would not be coming home. Why else would he have spoken to her the way he did when he flew overhead? She did not want to think about such an event.

Lying in her bed, sleep evaded her. As the dawn rose, Catherine heard the distant rumble of the aircraft returning. She jumped out of bed, slipped her clothes on and quietly crept out of the house. Once outside, she ran like the wind along the country lanes until she reached the spot where, just hours ago, she had watched the aircraft take off. Now she watched as they landed, quieter than when they took off. Slowly, wearily they taxied back to their dispersals, their crews tumbling silently out of the bellies and into the waiting trucks and buses. Catherine did not know if Tommy's aircraft had returned. She could not see any of the aircrew distinctly enough to recognise anyone. She wanted to call out to them, to ask them if S for Sugar had landed safely, but they were too far away to hear her.

"Tommy," she whispered. "Tommy, tell me you are safe." But Tommy did not answer.

Dragging herself home, Catherine felt sick. Her instinct told her that Tommy had not made it, but her heart did not want to believe it. Once home, Catherine's mother made tea and breakfast, but Catherine was not hungry. Of course Tommy is alright, said her heart, he always is. He will be at the pub this evening, you wait and see. But Catherine's head was answering differently.

"Perhaps the aircraft was shot down and the crew have all been taken prisoner," suggested Catherine's mother. "He will be alright. The war will be over for him. I'm sure you'll be getting a letter from him soon."

But Catherine's head would not accept that idea either.

Operating on automatic, Catherine worked at the assembly line in the local tank manufacturing factory, lost in her thoughts. She was glad that the place was so noisy. It made it almost impossible to speak to anyone as you could not hear each other. The girls had worked out their own form of sign language to be able to chat while working, but

Catherine managed to avoid any eye contact with her colleagues, and so avoid having to explain why she looked so unhappy. Some of the older women knew straight away what the problem was. They had seen many young girls fall in love with soldiers or airmen, only to have their hearts broken when the man got killed in action. They would leave Catherine alone for a few days to grieve, and then they would take her in hand, and liven her up a bit. There were lots of other young men to fall in love with.

But Catherine did not want to be cheered up. She did not want any other man to fall in love with. She was in love with Tommy, and he was in love with her. Two days later, Catherine plucked up the courage to go to the pub in the village. It was full of noisy, happy people. Catherine looked around for Tommy, or his crew. They were not there. She spotted a ginger haired young airman whom she had seen talking to Tommy some weeks ago. Perhaps he was on the same squadron, and could tell her what happened, she thought.

As she approached the man, he recognised her as Tommy Blond's girlfriend. He could see the questioning look in her eyes. He shifted uneasily. Obviously nobody had told her what had happened.

"Hello. I don't know if you know me, but…."

"Yes, I do know you," interrupted the young man. "You are Tommy Blond's girl. I'm sorry, very sorry. He was a great bloke."

Catherine gulped. *Was*. He used the past tense. Was. That means that Tommy is no more. Her eyes filled with tears. Catherine looked at the young man and asked what had happened.

"You don't want to know. It's better not to know."

"But I need to know, to be able to come to terms with everything," begged Catherine.

"They were shot down over Germany," said the young man, unable to look Catherine in the eye. "The plane was ripped in two. Hit the ground and blew up. They didn't stand a chance."

Catherine closed her eyes and the first tears rolled down her cheeks.

"Sorry," mumbled the young man, "These things happen."

He shuffled away to avoid any more questions. It was not good to go into detail about these things, especially when you were about to get airborne yourself that night.

Catherine slipped out of the pub into the cool night air. That was it then. Now she knew what had happened to Tommy. He was dead. Just as her head had tried to tell her heart. She made her way home, through the haze of tears, and into her mother's waiting arms. Her mother cradled Catherine's head, rocking her to and fro, as she sobbed long into the night.

Life was grey, a monotonous round of work, tears and sleep. Eventually, Catherine was able to accept that Tommy was dead. Looking at the photograph of him which she kept by her bedside, she remembered his voice that evening of his last flight. I love you, Catherine, he had said. Wait for me. Always.

"I will, Tommy. I will wait for you. Always," she whispered softly.

The war ended, life went back to normal, or at least as normal as it could be with towns demolished, and thousands of men killed, never to return. Rationing was still in force, food was scarce, times were tough. Catherine lost her job at the tank factory as there was no longer the demand for tanks. She managed to get a job at the local library. The quietness of the library was welcome after the noise of the factory. Catherine engrossed herself in the world of books, cataloguing and stacking books by day, and reading in the evenings. She did not care to go out. At first her parents were worried and tried to encourage their daughter to enjoy life more. But Catherine assured them that she was alright and did not need to go out to enjoy life.

The years rolled on. Catherine's parents died and she continued to live in the house where she had grown up. She did not feel that she was strange being a spinster although there were many who raised their eyebrows. She had dedicated her life to the library. The house was clean and the back garden was full of vegetables tended by her own hand. Vegetables always taste better when they are home grown, thought Catherine. In the front garden flowers bloomed from spring to autumn in a wide and vivid array of colours. Catherine won minor awards at garden fetes for her flowers and vegetables.

"You ought to be in hospital. This is quite a serious infection you have got. When you are in your eighties, as you are, these infections take a lot of beating." The doctor put away his stethoscope. "Have you got anyone popping in to keep an eye on you?"

"Oh, yes," lied Catherine. "I have a grand-niece who looks in every day."

"Good," replied the doctor, "I'll come back in a day or two, to see how you are doing."

"Thank you," Catherine smiled weakly. She listened as the doctor let himself out of the house. She leaned back into her pillows, coughing hoarsely. It is only a cold, she muttered to herself. I don't know what all the fuss is about. I must have caught it when I went for a walk in the rain. Everyone catches colds in the winter. As she had told the doctor, it was nothing. She did not mention how bad the coughing was, she did not want to waste the doctor's time. He had far more serious patients to look after. Tiredness overwhelmed her, and Catherine slept.

She was too weak to get out of bed to make herself anything to eat or drink. She was not hungry but she was thirsty. Nobody came to visit her or to help her. With a high temperature, dehydration and weariness, Catherine became delirious. Her chest ached from the coughing, her body was soaked in sweat, her breathing raspy and shallow. She was muttering to herself, half finished words.

Suddenly, there was a moment of clarity in her derision. Catherine opened her eyes, the room was dark. It must be night time. The coughing had stopped for a while and she could breathe reasonably normally. Gingerly, she sat up in bed. Her head swam and she thought she would pass out, but the feeling slowly ebbed. Carefully getting out of bed, Catherine slid her feet into her cold slippers and stood up. She felt very wobbly, but that was only natural, as she had been in bed for several days. Slowly, she inched forward, afraid that her legs would give way. But they held firm. Taking her dressing gown from the hook on the bedroom door, she wrapped it around herself. She had lost a lot of weight, and the gown almost wrapped itself twice around her body. Holding on to the banister, Catherine carefully descended the stairs.

The rush of cold air as she opened the door, almost swept Catherine off her feet. Oh, it felt good and smelled so sweet after the rancid atmosphere of her bedroom. Tentatively at first, then more confidently, Catherine walked down the path towards the gate, and into the lane. There was nobody about, she was alone. Slowly but determinedly Catherine walked along the leafy lane as she had done most evenings of her life. At the crossroads she turned right and walked towards the fence which was the boundary of the old airfield. Most of the airfield had long gone, an industrial estate having replaced many of the hangars and other buildings. Some of the concrete of the runway was still visible, although weeds grew chest high among the cracks. Catherine stood at the same place as she had done the night that Tommy Blond had taken off for his final flight. The same place where she stood most evenings. Everywhere was derelict and silent.

As she stood at the fence, the earth began to tremble. There was a rumbling noise. Looking across at the aircraft dispersals, Catherine could see the huge dark shapes of the Lancaster Bombers. She could see the ant-like people in comparison working underneath the great bellies of the beasts. Aircrew arrived in trucks and buses and climbed up the ladders into the black machines. As more engines were started up, the noise grew louder. The whiff of cordite and engine oil pricked Catherine's nostrils, the smoke caused her to cough.

Now, as the aircraft were ready to taxi out, the engines surged, the sound so loud that it hurt the eardrums. Catherine did not cover her ears, she had waited for so long to hear these sounds that she did not want to miss out on the experience. The ground shook beneath her feet. The big, black giants slowly taxied to the other end of the airfield, ready for take off.

One by one the Lancasters lumbered down the runway towards Catherine. Slowly they inched themselves into the air. As they flew over her head, Catherine waved at the crews. She could see them clearly, all the happy, smiling young men. Then S for Sugar thundered down the runway.

"I love you, Catherine," shouted Tommy Blond, waving. "Wait for me. Always."

"I will," Catherine shouted back, as the bomber skimmed overhead. "I will."

The Lancasters headed off towards their destination and slowly the noise subsided and the ground stopped moving.

Catherine sank down onto the grassy verge to wait for Tommy as she had promised. She felt exhausted. She could not keep her eyes open. As she drifted into sleep, she was vaguely aware that it had started to rain, a soft, quiet rain.

The sound of the aircraft engines pierced her sleep. Catherine awoke and opened her eyes. The rain was hitting her face hard, she was totally drenched, but she hardly noticed. The engine noise was getting louder. The boys were on their way back. Lying on her bed in the hedgerow, too weak to get up, Catherine heard the Lancasters flying overhead, turning for their landing. The ground vibrated to their sounds. She counted them as they flew over. All back. All safe and sound.

Turning her head, Catherine saw a man walking towards her. He was grinning from ear to ear.

"I knew you'd wait for me," he said, as he dropped down on the grass beside Catherine. He ran his hand through his blond hair, moving it out of his face, but it immediately fell forward again.

"Of course I waited. I promised, didn't I?"

"Come along, sweetheart. We have to go now." Tommy took Catherine by the hand. "We have a wedding to attend."

The waiting was finally over. Catherine looked into Tommy's face. She felt totally happy. She sank into her final sleep.

Come Here Often?   by   Katy Holderness

Sandra sat on the edge of the bed which was strewn with clothes, her bemused husband Peter stood in the doorway and smiled.

"What's up love can't find a thing to wear again?"

"Oh I don't know, which one should I wear? The black or navy?" sighed Sandra.

"And what's wrong with the red one, I like you in that" said Peter pointing to a strawberry red coloured dress thrown on the floor.

"Yes, so do I but would it look right today, I don't want to look the odd one out, what do you think Steve would say?" muttered Sandra.

"Today I don't think he would mind either way" shrugged Peter.

"Oh, you're no use at all, just leave me alone and I'll decide myself and why you can't come with me I don't know, Steve is one of your best friends after all and what about Mary?" muttered Sandra.

"Oh, don't go on, I thought you of all people would understand I told you what I had to do, it's the first race of the season today and Steve's got a good batch of birds this year, some sure winners. I've had quiet word with Mary and she's fine about it and told her not to worry I would be at the shindig afterwards" said Peter.

"Yes, I thought you might be, anywhere where there's free drink about. I'm sure you think more about them blooming pigeons than you do of me" shouted Sandra.

"Hey, come on now, this is for Steve, remember? And mates don't break promises and I promised him I would be here when his best bluey Matilda comes in so I can clock her. Anyway, if the wind stays as it is she'll be blown home before the do even starts and I could honour you with my presence" laughed Peter.

"Oh, you." said Sandra throwing a pillow at him.

....

"You Hoo, Sandy, over here."

Sandra turned around and her heart did a double somersault, for there running towards her like an overly dressed clown in fluorescent pink and green was Edna the school Lollipop lady, she really had a heart of gold and would do anything for anybody, she knew all the children's and parent's names, grandparents too, she knew everyone, in fact she knew everything about everybody. As Edna ran, her rolls of fat wibble wobbled about, her orange hair and bright pink lipstick clashed vividly with the multi coloured coat she wore, breathlessly, she caught up with Sandra.

"Why I didn't know you were coming today, Pete not with you?" said Edna stretching her neck.
Sandra didn't want to explain about the pigeons so just shook her head.

"Oh, pity about that, if we'd known we could have all come together couldn't we George and shared the car?" she said shouting to her husband.

"Yes dear." said her embarrassed spouse.

"Well, if you don't mind me saying, this does make a nice change doesn't it? You know, being amongst friends and the like. Oh, I'm so pleased you've come now; we can catch up on all the news. and if there's room we can all sit together can't we. Come here often do you?" enquired Edna

"No sorry only been twice this year." muttered Sandra in a somewhat apologetic way.

"Oh, only a couple of times you say, shame that isn't it George? I said it's a shame. I've been seven or eight times so far and it's only the beginning of October could make it ten before the years out if I'm lucky. George likes to come to but can't always make it, can you love, can't get the time off work you see, I suppose your Pete's the same isn't he?" said Edna straightening her husband's tie.

Sandra was dumfounded and just nodded, giving an involuntary shudder as they approached the large impressive building, Edna noticed and gave her arm a quick squeeze.

"I always say this is one of the best bits, the not knowing of what's going to happen" said Edna as she pushed open the ornate glass doors, with Sandra and George following closely behind her.   .

" Well, just as I thought not much room left, I told you George we should have come earlier but you would insist on having that extra cuppa." fumed Edna as she looked around and saw the place was already quite full, then spying a space she elbowed her way onto an already crowded bench.

"Right George you sit on the end, and then Sandy and I'll sit here. Now then, are we all settled?" said Edna as she eased her ample body into the space much to the discomfort of the person she had almost sat on. "Sorry love, bit of a squeeze isn't it? Why if it isn't our Mavis, don't mind if I park me backside here do you?" asked Edna, the lady in question squirmed in her seat. "But I couldn't be doing with standing all the time not with me legs the way they are. Been giving me some gip lately I can tell you, it's the standing about in all weathers that does it. Oh, I say, have you seen the flowers over there, don't they look grand, I bet it's that new woman Mrs. Patterson that's done them, well it wouldn't be old Gladys, no, not with her fingers the way they are, real bad they are all knotted and bulging out"

George looked at Sandra giving her a little smile.

Edna, glimpsing another friend called out loudly. "Hiya, Janice, how's your mum's hip now she's been done? Coping alright is she? You been in for your piles op yet? No? Sandy here had them done a couple of month's back, proper poorly she was weren't you love?" Edna thumped Sandra's arm heartily.

"Edna be quiet." George seethed.

"Well, I was only being neighbourly that's all" muttered Edna as she flipped open the gold fastener on her rather large lime green handbag.

Silence, then the first strands of music emerged, Sandra shut her eyes and let the soothing sounds ease her aching head and wondered if Matilda had arrived home yet when she was rudely awakened by the rustling of paper as Edna handed her a sticky toffee, which she refused and watched in amazement as the crumpled bag was passed back along the row.

"Sorry love, can't take her anywhere" muttered George to Sandra as he covered his face with his hands.

The music faded softly away, a sign that everyone was to stand up and a distinguished cloaked figure loomed up in front of the crowded room.

"Why, if it isn't our John." said Edna excitedly as she dug Sandra in the ribs. "I knew his dad; he was good at this sort of thing as well. Told you it would be a good one today." smiled Edna sucking noisily on her toffee.

Then the said John's voice boomed out loud and clear.

"Dearly Beloved, we are gathered here today in the House of God, to say a final farewell to our dear Departed brother Steven …………"

The Early Morning Callers by   Katy Holderness

"Hey up, Nance, what yer doing?"

"Leave me be."

"Oh, me head".

Ted rolled over to see why his wife was so intent on pulling his pyjama jacket off, but she was fast asleep, her new blue rinse perm snugly encased in its fishnet cage, snoring as usual like a steam train.

"What the".… Ted sat bolt upright.

By the light of the moonlight streaming through the half drawn curtains he could see what appeared to be two work men, well they looked like work men, togged up in their overalls and caps, one of which carried a clip board and the other a brief case.

"What the hell are you doing in my bedroom?" roared Ted.

The one holding the clipboard read from his notes.

"You are Edward (Ted, Teddy) Moore born 4th November 1923. No. 704568S/5, mother - Alice Maude, Father - William Edward, Brother - of Percy, Walter, James, and Annie, you married Muriel Nancy Smith on 10th May 1950, father of six, grandfather of four and great grandfather of one. That correct?"

"Yea, except I've only got five kids" said Ted.

"Sorry sir, but it says six here and now everything's done on computer it can't be wrong" said the clipboard man pointing his finger to the numbers as he held it out for Ted to see.

"Well, I'm telling yer, I've only got five kids and I should knows, there's Michael, Patrick, Anthony, Peter and young Johnny, one, two, three, four, five" said an indignant Ted.

"Well, we'll have to look into that, Archie make a note of that" said the clipboard holder to his partner. Archie opened his brief case and took out a pad and pencil.

"But apart from that minor discrepancy the other facts are correct?"

"Yes, but yer still ain't explained who yer are and why yer in me bedroom" said Ted now sitting up right.
The one with the clipboard replied.

"Well, I'm Seth and this here is Archie, been sent by our Foreman Gabe to fetch you in, your times up."

"I knew it, I knew should never have had that last whiskey chaser, me brains twaddled."

"Ah, out celebrating were we?" asked Archie.

"Yea, I just become a great granddad, a girl at last after all them lads aye, a real little princess she is" sighed Ted.

"We've been wetting the little lass's head down at the Legion."

"Well, need we say more? That's it, one in, one out, can't have too many down here, too crowded be half already." said Seth.

"Yer can't mean it's time for me to pop me clogs?

Why I ain't been ill, fit as a fiddle I am. Just look what I've been doing today. First thing I were planting me early tates, made me sweat a bit I must admit but I were alright. Then I helps the Missus put on a bit of a spread for the family, yer know sandwiches and a bit of cake befores we goes down to the Legion for a bit of a shin dig with all our mates. And I knows I only had 4 pints and that whiskey chaser our Johnny bought me, so I knows I ain't drunk. Hey, Nancy, yer silly moo wake up. If I were yer bleeding cat, yer'd be up like a shot."
Ted shouted at his sleeping wife.

"Sorry old chap. But it says here in black and white you've got to come in on 1ˢᵗ April, 2005 at 4.00a.m." said Archie.

"Ah, well, I've got another ten minutes, because that there clock is ten minutes fast so there." said
Ted with a smug grin on his face as he looked at the illuminated clock face on the dressing table.

"Now, come on it's not so bad" said Seth. "You'll meet all your old mates."

"Yea and me enemies." butted in Ted.

"No, it's not like that, everyone is mates where we are. Aren't they Archie, I said we're all mates?"

Archie nodded as he concentrated on unravelling the long reams of computer print outs from his brief case.

"Don't suppose there's any chance of a mistake is there?" muttered Ted pulling the sheet up to his chin.

"Not the slightest chance. We have the best technology that money can buy, a computer that can tell you anything you want in seconds and a lovely girl by the name of Gloria operates it, a real little whiz kid." said Seth smugly.

"Ah, but don't forget in the past we have had one or two hiccups, when we've had to bring them back" said Archie handing Seth a sheet of paper.

"Well yes I do remember, but that doesn't really count - it was ages ago and it wasn't really Mary's fault, she should have had her eyes tested earlier but she could never get an appointment at the opticians they were always booked up." said Seth.

"Oh, you just carry on chatting don't mind me, I just lives here" said Ted now annoyed and folding his arms in front of him.

"Sorry old boy. Now come on tell me, what's your favourite music?" asked Archie.

"Well, me and the Missus we likes the Oldies, yer know Glenn Miller, the big band sounds, we used to knock em dead with our jitterbugging.
Then Nance were also very partial to Buddy Holly, but he looked like a bit of a nancy boy to me"

"Say, no more. Come on in Glenn and Bud." Archie clicked his fingers. With a whirr and a bang and a cloud of smoke there before him stood Glenn Miller and Buddy Holly. Ted rubbed his eyes.

"Howdy Ted, nice ter see yer" Glenn held out his hand.

"Not so sure about the nancy bit though" said Buddy leaning towards him with a grin.

"Yer for real then?" whispered Ted.

"Sure are" said Buddy. "Real cool."

"Right" Archie said. Let's have a twirl at some tunes." The bedroom was soon filled with the sound of music.

Glenn and Buddy did a couple of tunes each.

"Listen Nance this is for us. *American Patrol*. Glenn Miller, remember? Gawd, I can't believe it, she still ain't moved. Are yer deaf woman?"

"Sorry Ted, she can't hear you, not her time yet. Now then old chap are you going to come quietly?" said Seth.

"I can't go, not yet. Well, me and Nance well we ain't been apart for a night since we were wed, we belongs together. And any road I got a bet on the horses tomorrow, the 2.30 at Aintree, Shining Light, it's a cert for sure." Ted clung to the bed head as Seth and Archie stepped forward their arms out stretched.

"No, I ain't going anywhere, somebody help me"
Glenn & Buddy gave him the thumbs up.

"See you real soon" they chorused.

"Gawd help me" shouted Ted.

"No good calling him" said Archie. "He's away on an assertive course."

Suddenly there was a crash of thunder and the bedroom was illuminated with a bright orange light.

"STOP! …Wrong one…."

"Heavens above. It's Gabe" said Archie.

"Gabriel is the name" …….. boomed a voice from the light.

"Sorry" muttered Archie.

Seth studied his clipboard as his employers voice droned on.

"We have again had a little misdemeanour but nothing that can't be rectified. Gloria poor child has come down with the most terrible head cold and we have had to bring Mary out of retirement to take over the reins, but it is most unfortunate she doesn't seem to be able to grasp even the simplest of instructions these days and has mixed up many of the incoming dates, we have quite a task on our hands trying to sort things out and consequently we have had to close down the computer until further notice, Mary will of course be severely reprimanded this time. Now come along you two, we have a lot of work to catch up on" commanded Gabriel.

Archie quickly stuffed his papers back into his briefcase and Seth put his clip board under his arm before giving Ted a salute and heading towards the window.

"Hoy, wait a minute" shouted Ted his heart beating loudly as he saw where Seth and Archie were going.

"My dear chap. My most sincere apologies. I am so sorry we have troubled you and caused you any inconvenience. Please try and forget about this most unfortunate episode. We'll bid you a very good night and pleasant dreams." said Gabriel from the dimming light.

Shaking his head and rubbing his eyes Ted stared towards the open window.

"Oh, and by the way Mr. Moore, I should change your bet for the 2.30 to Charlie's Angels!" said Gabriel as the room suddenly plunged into darkness..."

The Picnic   by   Katy Holderness

"Well Gladys what do yer think to me new perm? Our Maureen did it for me" said Maude to her friend as she preened herself in the little car's mirror.

"Oh, very nice" said Gladys pushing Maude out of the way and adjusting her driving mirror, looking behind her and then at the mirror tutting as she did so.

"Any road it's a lovely day for a picnic, hope the weather holds. I brought me brolly just in case and me big coat, as yer knows it gets a bit chilly like up Sutton Bridge way, but it'll be nice ter see some greenery though won't it? I does like me flowers, but they don't like me, always dies on me they do, I has the death wish on me. Oh, but our Gwen got me some lovely artificial ones they looks a real treat, have yer seen them I put them in me front room window?"

"Maude will yer give over prattling on, yer can see I'm trying to concentrate and get me mirrors right. And for gawd's sake get yer head out of the way" said an agitated Gladys.

"Well there's no need to get mardy. And why yer didn't want to go on the bus like the rest of the club I don't know" said Maude settling her large frame back into her seat and trying to de-tangle the seat belts.

"Yer knows why, I wants a quick escape if I have to, what with our Murtal giving birth at any time. I needs to be on hand like. Our Norman promised he'd ring on the mobile if there's any news.Here you hold it. Any road you could have gone with them and sat with Alice, I's quite capable on me own yer know" huffed Gladys thrusting the phone into Maude's hands.

Maude took the mobile phone and sat staring at it.

"What a load of hassle over a blooming cat" muttered Maude.

"What's that you say?" reared up Gladys.

"Nowt. Nowt. Just thinking out loud. I hopes yer don't expect me to do owt with this here contraption, I don't like them, causes brain trouble yer know, and what with Norm and all his problems well I'm surprised he wanted one" said Maude gingerly turning it over in her hands, as if it would explode at any minute.

"Well, it were our Pauline, she bought it for me.

Worried she were if owt happened, while I was out in Wally alone." said Gladys fondly patting the car's dashboard, then taking a duster she gave the windscreen a quick rub before taking a final look out of all the windows.

"Now, then Maude, yer did put the hamper to the left hand side and that bag of potatoes to the right, I likes to level the weight out yer know, equal like." said Gladys.

"Yes, of course, I knows what I'm at" said Maude folding her arms and holding the mobile upright.

"Right then, we'll be off…

Why, just look at that, did yer see them grandsons of yours, young George and Sidney? I just seen them jump over Riley's fence, well I never" said Gladys, revving the engine and grating the gears.

"Best be safe than sorry with your driving" said Maude as she was flung towards the dashboard, she were sure her grandsons had made the sign of the cross as she waved back at them.

Maude thought it was amazing that they managed to arrive at Sutton Bridge Park without a major incident, well it didn't really count when they went round that last roundabout three times, or going over them there bumpy pebbles after nearly missing their turning for the park. Mind you it were a little worrying when they overtook that car and caravan and there were that big lorry coming towards them, but nowt much else. Maude gave a silent prayer of thanks to her Maker for her safe deliverance.

"I'll just park Wally up here, on the high like away from all those buses, then we'll go and find the others" said Gladys.

"I'll bring the food, here you have this here phone, gives me the willies it does" said Maude handing Gladys the mobile, before hauling herself out of the car and rubbing her aching legs.

"Oh, me poor old pins"

"Oh give over Maude we ain't been on the road much over an hour. Now get the hamper out and I'll lock me baby up. Aye yer were right about bringing our coats it's a bit nippy" said Gladys doing up her gabardine mac.
Maude pushed the seat forward to retrieve the hamper and struggled to get it out of the tight space.

"Good heavens Gladys, what yer packed, it weighs a blooming ton" said Maude putting the wicker basket over a plump arm.

"Well, I knows yer likes yer food and I put that bottle of Napoleon brandy in, just to ward off the cold for later. Funny I thought Norm would have rung, at least to let me know Murtal were alright" said Gladys looking at her phone.

"Well, yer know him, man of few words, probably don't want to waste money on a call if nowt were happening, any road, put it away now. Oh, Look Glad, I sees Alice and the others over there, looks like they've just arrived." said Maude pointing a chubby finger towards the bus park.

"Come on I'm proper parched, a nice cuppa wouldn't come amiss." Maude took the arm of her friend and led her down the gentle slope towards the rest of the For-Get-Me-Not Club for the over 60's.

"I think I'll leave this here basket on the bus with the others and collect it later, can't be lugging this weight around all day what with me bad legs and all" said Maude letting go of Gladys and making towards the gravelled coach park area. Gladys sighed and put the silent phone carefully into her coat pocket.

"Ah, that's better, I thought me arm were dead" said Maude as she handed her hamper to a somewhat disgruntled coach driver grimacing as she flexed her fingers to get the circulation back into her arm. "Come along Glad get a move on, just look at that there queue " Maude got hold of Gladys's arm again and tugged her towards a small wooden hut that was advertising refreshments.

The steady stream of visitors were already quickly filling the grubby plastic tables and chairs that lined the perimeter of the building.

"You get a table and I'll get the drinks" said Maude as she pushed Gladys towards a couple of vacant chairs and marched off in the direction of the long queue.Gladys took the phone out of her pocket again and looked mournfully at it. Still Norman hadn't rung, she supposed she could ring him, but best not, he could have one of his head's on. No best leave it.

"Here Glad get hold of this here cup. Still mooning over that there phone I see. For Gawds sake put it down and get this down yer. You would not believe the prices, daylight robbery, one fifty, just for a couple of cups of tea."

said Maude spilling some into the saucers as she spoke. Gladys lay the phone on the table and tutted as she took a paper hankie and wiped her saucer dry, while Maude much to her disgust just tipped hers back into her cup and sat down puffing and panting.

"It's no good Maude yer'll have to do summat about yer weight, like yer doctor said, it can't be doing yer heart any good " said Gladys looking at the red face of her friend. Maude shrugged her shoulders and blew on her tea.

"Any road, while I was waiting in that queue I had a quick word with Alice, says she's not feeling too bad today, I asked her if she wanted to come round with us but she thought it wouldn't look right not when she's been sat with Edna all morning, I says ok love and we'd catch up later. I'm really pleased she's looking better" Maude paused for breath as she took another slurp of her tea. "I fancied a bit of Madeira but I weren't paying what they were asking, no I'll wait for me dinner. What yer put in the sandwiches Glad, summat nice I hope?"

"Oh, how can you think of food at a time like this, when my poor Murtal could be in pain and agony somewhere." sniffed Gladys, taking the tea - dampened tissue to wipe her eyes.

"Sorry love, but yer know me" said Maude staring into her tea.

"Yes, blooming self all the time, I knows yer don't like cats but yer could have a bit more consideration at a time like this" fumed Gladys.

"Sorry" muttered Maude.

"Any road its nice to see Alice getting out and about again, a couple of a days ago I didn't think she would make it, yer know it were a real bad batch of flu she had. And maybe she's getting more settled into that new bungalow of hers now" said Gladys, drumming her fingers on the table top.

"Aye, I hopes so, but I wouldn't have gone up Morton's Copse, even if everything were brand new. No not away from all me mates and everything, yer know it would be that daughter of hers doing, bossy little madam that she is. Any road I thinks I has enough with me Grankids without worrying about blooming animals thank you very much, as you'd know if your Pauline had caught. Never a minute to me self sometimes, that's why's I enjoys coming out on these do's, escape from it all" said Maude still smarting as she looked around her peaceful surroundings.

"Well, we's got ham, tongue and pickle in sandwiches if yer must know, bit of salad, pork pie, apple pies and Norman sent yer a piece of his fruit slab, he knows I can't eat it cause raisins upsets me innards but he knows yer likes it. That suit her Ladyship?" said Gladys.

"Ohh, that's just grand Glad" said Maude licking her lips.

"Any road it's not our Pauline's fault she ain't caught, summat to do wiv her pipes so doctors say and you shouldn't be so bleeding soft with them kids of yours, why yer've had yer own, up to them to look after their own, I'd tell them. And talking about blooming animals as yer calls them, if I remembers rightly not so long ago we had that there escapade with your George's hamster and not to mention his dog!" said Gladys still annoyed with her friend. Maude coloured up. "Aye well, that weren't my fault, well not really. Yer just wait till yer gets them grandkids of yer own somehow yer just gets involved with things without trying. Any road, Grandkids are all but grown up now except young George, and Carrot Top, I loves them all but they worries me to death with their problems, great grandkids next shouldn't wonder, then more problems. Yer only had your Pauline didn't yer?"

"Yes, of course I did" snapped back Gladys.

A bit too quickly thought Maude as she stared thoughtfully at her friend.

Maude and Gladys had grown up together, living in the same street, same schools, lived in each others' pockets for years, like Siamese twins their mam's said, never apart.Gladys got work at that posh dress shop in town and Maude started at the local bakery, with all that lovely fresh bread and cakes. Everything were going alright for the pair of them, Maude had started walking out with young Ted the new dough maker at the bakery, and Gladys with Bert Smith's older brother Johnny, bit too old for her Maude had thought and so did Bert who had hung his heart out for her. Then one night when Ted was walking home late because he had been working on a special wedding order, he had told Maude about the terrible row coming from the Smith's house, heck of a noise there were, next morning they heard Johnny had packed his bags there and then and cleared out, it were rumoured he went off to join the army, or gone abroad. Bert had gained a lovely shiner, their poor mam cried for days and Johnny's name were never mentioned again and neither hide nor hair of him had ever been heard since.

Then there were that funny thing about Gladys having to go to stay with her Aunty Vera in Blackpool soon after, cos she caught scarlet fever or summat like that, bit quick like, why she must've bin gone a year or more, funny thing that.

Any road, now't were said when she came back, but she weren't the same lass as before, not quite so cocky. Then she met her Norman, he were a work mate with Ted down at bakery and it somehow seemed right that they got together and it weren't long after before they were hitched. Soft as grease he were with her and still is, aye, it must be neigh on fifty years now and she never did let on about her seaside jaunt.

Funny old world, thought Maude. She drank her tea in silence, staring at Gladys still holding on to her phone. "Come on then Glad can't sit here maudlin, times getting on" said a refreshed Maude standing up and looking around her at the beautiful countryside and thinking hows it made a nice change from the rows of grubby terraced streets they were used to.

Maude and Gladys spent the next couple of hours savouring the delights of the many floral displays of Sutton Park meandering along its many winding paths and watching the little ducklings swimming about on the lake in and out of the water lilies and bull rushes, the Spring sunshine shone brightly, forming hundreds of rainbows on the greeny blue waters.

Approaching yet another turning, the pair spied a gift shop selling not only novelties but cut flowers and plants.

"Isn't everything so lovely, I'm going to take me home a keepsake" said Gladys.

"Well I ain't. I just likes to look at them, all very nice but they'd be dead before I gets home. I'll get me self a few toffees, share them out with the bairns later." said Maude picking up a very large multi coloured tin, tucking it under her arm as she spoke.

"Oh, yes Maude this will look lovely in me front room, match me wallpaper, what do you think?" said Gladys holding a bright pink arrangement out in front of her.

"Yes, very nice, I'm sure. Now, come on let's see what yer've packed in that there hamper, me stomach thinks me throat's bin cut" said Maude rushing towards the coach with no sign of her bad legs now. Feeling a little miffed, as she had to wait her turn for the others to get their hampers off first.

"Well, only fair really Maude, we didn't travel with them now did we, they's only minding it for us" said Gladys putting her plant down on the ground and again looking at the silent phone.

"I keeps telling yer he'll ring when summat's happened" said Maude hauling the basket towards her from the boot of the coach. "Here, give us a hand, I'm sure it's got heavier. Let's go over to them there trees, near the lake, where's we can see the little ducks and get a bit of cover." said Maude pointing a podgy finger towards the water and a couple of wooden benches.

They took the basket between them, Gladys still holding tightly onto the mobile phone and glaring at it as though willing it to ring, Maude puffed her way towards one of the benches. She was now clearly out of breath and sat down with a thud.

"Gawd, Glad I'm fair whacked, I think I'll have a drop of the hard stuff if yer don't mind" said
Maude, but before she could take the lid off the hamper, a loud voice rudely interrupted her.

"Attention, Attention, will the owner of a yellow mini registration number WAL 278Y please come to the main entrance at once where we have an emergency…"

"Oh, Gladys, that's yer Wally, what's to be now" said Maude looking at a worried Gladys.

"I don't know. Come on best find out, leave that there." stammered Gladys as Maude stared longingly at the food basket.

Gladys helped Maude to her feet but as they turned to trudge back up the sloping path, there came loud shouts and screaming.

"Get out of the way!"
"Move yourselves!"
"Stand to the side!"

"Help!"

"Runaway car!"

"Wally!"

Gladys and Maude were mesmerized as the little car came trundling past them and as though watching a slow motion picture stared in amazement as it slid into the water amongst a clump of bull rushes. The pair clung onto each other. What on earth were they to do now?

"Get the Napoleon " They said in union.

Turning round towards the bench, Gladys cried out as if in pain, Maude was alarmed.

"Gawd, now what?" said Maude.

"A miracle, Maude, a bleeding miracle." said Gladys excitedly.

"What!" said Maude.

"It's Murtal, my baby." said Gladys as she saw her beloved cat climb out of the hamper basket.

"Come to mummy, let me look at you. Oh, Maude, look, there are four little Murtals" said Gladys in awe, now clearly forgetting about the fate of her poor Wally.

"Charming" said a disgruntled Maude as she looked at the new off spring nestling amongst the ham, tongue and pickle sandwiches as her stomach rumbled loudly.

The Great Lincolnshire Challenge   by   Paul Stafford

"You must be mad!" taunted Geoff, cosseted by the warmth of his car, as Louise struggled by herself to lift down her heavy bicycle from the back of the vehicle. She shivered as the cold wind froze her bare legs.

"Cycle 100 miles in a day, Skegness and back, huh, I reckon by the time you get to Wragby, you'll be ringing me to come and get you," he jibed from the inside of the car, parked on double yellow lines on Lincoln's Bailgate.

Louise finally succeeded in unloading the bike. Totally ignoring her husband, she wheeled it past the front of the White Hart and round the corner by the Magna Carta. "I will do it, just to spite you," she muttered, but the comment wasn't reflected in the deep echoing in her mind. Perhaps she wouldn't even be able to cycle the 10 miles to reach Wragby!

As she passed under the arch at the entrance to the Lincoln Cathedral forecourt, she recounted that in fifteen years of marriage he had constantly put her down. She was so determined to show him she could complete the Challenge.

Louise looked at the magnificent west front of the Cathedral. By the steps she saw   three other cyclists who were going to be doing the 100-mile Challenge with her. What she didn't know was like her, each of them was very worried about what lay ahead.

Playing impatiently with his cycle computer was Ben, a 26-year-old solicitor. Tall with dark curly hair, he wore a matching dark blue cycle top and lycra shorts. Ben was thinking about all the people who had agreed to sponsor him to cycle from Lincoln to Skegness and back. He desperately needed to raise money to send his teenage brother to America for urgent medical attention. He had to finish the Challenge today.

Emma, an attractive third year Lincoln University student, was nervously adjusting her helmet. Her long blonde hair was getting caught in the straps. She was tentatively stretching her legs that had been badly broken two years ago, when a bus had struck her while she was out running. Her face had been deeply scarred in the accident, leaving her short of any confidence. Finishing the 100-mile challenge today would be a tremendous boost.

Making mechanical adjustments to the gears on his cycle was Peter. He'd been cycling for over 25 years, since he was a teenager. He was worried about his appearance in court the following day. It might be a long time before he saw the Lincolnshire countryside again. He was determined make the most of the opportunity offered by the challenge.

The four cyclists had been drawn together by the article about Ben in the local paper. The piece had explained why Ben was doing the challenge. The editor had asked for other cyclists to volunteer. Ben had not been in favour of this idea at all, but as the paper had generously agreed to sponsor him, he had little option but to go along with what the editor wanted.

Apart from one meeting in the Magna Carta, where the four of them had agreed the route and discussed other logistics, they'd never met before.

Ben had set his cycle computer and now looked critically at the three other cyclists. He wasn't impressed. The older man's bike was a wreck. The dark haired woman was wearing a loose tee shirt and baggy shorts, more appropriate for a walk in the country than a 100-mile cycle ride. Worse still, the blonde couldn't even get her helmet on!

"What a shower," he muttered under his breath. He knew he should have argued harder with the editor. These three were going to hold him back!

Then the cathedral bell rang seven times on the chill, overcast, early June morning. The four cyclists were ready to undertake the Great Lincolnshire Challenge. Would the day end in glorious triumph or unmitigated disaster?

On hearing the bell chime Ben mounted his bike. He was very keen to get started. Peter though was staring at Emma, dressed in her skintight cycling top. She was most appealing. It was a pity about the scar across her face though. Emma turned away from him, realising what a long day she'd have at the back of the group avoiding his unwanted attention.

Louise noticed this. Nobody gave her a second glance anymore and sensed she might be the odd one out. The other three all had various types of racing cycles. Her basic bike, with a wicker basket on the front handlebars, seemed out of place. When Ben said that they'd have to average 12mph to complete the challenge before dark, she was panic-stricken. She'd never done anything like this speed before. When he said the first stop would be in Horncastle, Louise realised she'd have to cycle 10 miles past Wragby, before she could have her first rest!

Ben selected a gear on his red Dawes cycle, and rode off down Bailgate and under the Newport Arch. Louise pedalled hard to follow him. Emma pretended to alter her saddlebag, so Peter was forced to move off. Emma was therefore at the back, just what she wanted.

Ben had gone off at a quick pace and by the time he had reached the ring road there was a gap opening between him and the others. He reluctantly stopped at the roundabout to wait.

"Come on, we'll never make it," he chided, looking straight at Louise, as the others finally arrived. Louise was already red in the face and out of breath.

"You're going too fast for us," panted Louise.

"You mean too fast for you," Peter interjected, as he adjusted his saddle that had come loose on his 20-year-old rusting racer. Louise looked as if she would burst into tears at the rebukes. She was determined to keep going though.

The group kept quite close to each other for the next few miles, with Louise pedalling for all she was worth. At Langworth, Peter slowed suddenly, and Emma swerved to avoid running into the back of him. In doing so she fell off her bike and landed in a heap on the grass verge at the side of the road. Ben heard the clatter of bike hitting tarmac, looked back and saw what had happened.

Frustrated at another delay, Ben surveyed the scene. Emma was now back on her feet but massaging her legs, she looked close to tears. Peter was closely examining his faulty brakes.

Ben looked briefly at Emma "No damage to you then," then turned and pointed at Peter's bike, "but I'm not sure about that antique."

" Prat," muttered Peter as he got to work with his small spanners.

For Louise, the enforced break was a blessing, as she found a wooden bench and had a drink from her water bottle. The sun was starting to come out from behind the clouds.

Fifteen minutes later as the nearby Stainton church clock struck eight, Peter had sorted the problem, and the group were ready to go again.

"About time," moaned Ben.

"I'll lead with YOU behind me," Emma pointed to Ben. "I'm going nowhere near him and that decrepit thing."

Peter ignored the insult; his eyes were locked on Emma's tight lycra shorts as she remounted her bike. With Emma leading but unsure about her legs, the group travelled at a more sedate pace for the next few miles. It was a chance for Louise to take a breather, and for Peter to fiddle with his unpredictable gears. As they rolled through the picturesque Wragby marketplace, Louise gave a little cheer. At least Geoff wouldn't be picking her up from here. Only Ben was frustrated at the slow pace. He wanted to press on to be sure of finishing and raising the money.

Gradually Emma felt confident enough on her smart new cycle to increase the pace, although she was still wary that her legs would let her down. The accident had happened when she had been out jogging and the bus had hit her. Her University running career destroyed. A point well made by her legal team when the case went to court.

A specialist had suggested cycling as an alternate form of exercise and the hundred-mile challenge today was a major part of her rehabilitation. The fall she had suffered back down the road was upsetting.

She hadn't expected any compassion, but hoped that Ben might have cared. He was a fit looking guy, and she admired him for trying to raise the money to save his brother's life. Conscious of Ben's single-minded determination to finish the 100 miles, she pushed harder on her pedals.

As the pace increased, a gap opened between Emma and Ben and the other two. Peter might have overtaken Louise, but he could think of far worse things to do on a Sunday morning than cycle behind her shapely bottom.

Having sorted his bike out, he was now thinking about tomorrow and his appearance in court. Since his wife Jackie had gone off with her boss, the Child Support Agency had pursued him relentlessly over his contributions for their teenage kids. This had left him unable to pay his other bills, so he had stopped handing over the maintenance. He'd defaulted against the court order twice and had been warned about the serious consequences if he did it again. Three weeks ago he'd failed to pay the money over and so he'd received a summons. As the sun shone brightly as they cycled past Crowder's Nurseries, Peter wondered if he'd be locked up in the darkness of Lincoln Prison tomorrow night.

Emma and Ben had already been in "Myers Cafe" just off Horncastle Market Place for over ten minutes, when Peter and Louise eventually arrived. Emma had bought the teas and flapjacks and had tried to make conversation with Ben. He appeared engrossed in thought, Emma thought he was ignoring her. Ever since the accident, with the hideous scar on her face, good-looking guys didn't want to know her.

Ben was actually thinking about his young teenage brother Charlie, who had a brain tumour. Doctors at Lincoln and Sheffield hospitals had pronounced it incurable. Ben had heard that a Texas hospital was pioneering a new treatment. He had made contact with a doctor involved in the treatment, and who had agreed to operate on Charlie. The cost though was enormous, and his widowed mother was in no position to help. In a couple of years he might be able to afford the treatment, once he'd cleared his own university debts, but that would be too late for Charlie. Ben needed the money now, and even if he managed to finish the challenge today, he'd be several thousand pounds short.

Peter and Louise sat down at another table, and drank their cold drinks. Louise was very red in the face. She glanced across at the other two, with Emma sitting by Ben's side trying to engage him in conversation.

"Thanks for waiting for us," Louise sarcastically called across the café. Ben didn't respond.

"Far too slow" replied Emma hoping to win approval from Ben.

Louise looked at Peter "At least you waited for me, I know I'm not fast but I'll keep going." He smiled, but appeared to have something more important on his mind. "What a talkative bunch we are!" exclaimed Louise. She went off to the loo to wash her face.

When she returned the others were on their way out of the café. Emma was adjusting her shorts while Peter gawped at her; she gave him an angry look in return. Ben announced that the next bit was uphill. Louise groaned. That was all she wanted.

Leaving Horncastle, they started to climb through High Toynton and then turned off the main road to cycle towards Mavis Enderby. By now Ben and Peter had forged ahead but suddenly Emma's legs really started to hurt and she was forced to struggle along with Louise.

"I suppose we ought to wait," said Ben as they entered the village, "but at this rate we won't finish until tomorrow night," he moaned.

Peter looked worried. "That would mean a big problem for me."

Ben looked quizzically at him "Why's that?"

As they waited for the two women to catch up, Peter explained his situation.

"Mmm, big problem, can't really see how you can get out of that one, but I'll have a think about it," Ben responded. "Problem of your own making though," he added unhelpfully. Just then Emma and Louise came into view, both looked shattered.

After another ten-minute stop, during which Ben constantly looked at his watch, they started towards Spilsby. Ben was leading, Louise behind him, followed by Peter with Emma, who had to fend off an angry wasp, at the back. They crossed the busy A16 and cycled along through the pretty villages of Halton Holegate and Great Steeping, then suddenly in the quiet countryside just past Irby in the Marsh, Emma's front tyre felt soft and she slowed. She had a puncture! Desperately she called out but only Peter appeared to hear her. The other two had gone around a corner and were out of sight.

Emma felt real fear as Peter turned back towards her. She was totally alone with this man who had stared at her body at every opportunity. Her bike was useless. She couldn't run fast anymore. The other two were out of shouting distance. What could she do?

Suddenly she no longer heard the birds singing. The sun had passed under a dark black cloud. She stood, rooted to the spot as this man laid his bike down and strode purposely towards her.

"Have you punctured love? That's most unfortunate isn't it?" Emma thought a sly smile played across his face. He licked his lips. She was panic-stricken.

"Suppose you haven't got a spare inner tube, have you?" he asked. Emma shook her head numbly.

"Well it's a good job that I have, on this decrepit thing!" he pointed to his bike. "Now let's get you sorted out."

Emma watched in astonishment as clearly practiced hands took off the tyre, and pulled out the inner tube. Peter found the hole in the tube almost immediately. Taking out a new inner tube from the bag on his bike, he pumped it up slightly and placed it round Emma's wheel. Then he replaced the tyre and pumped in more air. With some pride, he lifted up Emma's now roadworthy bike.

"There you are, all ready to run again." He had repaired the puncture in less than five minutes. "Nice new bike this, bet it cost a pretty penny."

Emma was speechless. She was safely on her cycle again. Peter too had mounted his cycle. Both started pedalling.

Emma suddenly felt very foolish. Soon they had caught up with the others, and Ben asked what happened. Emma explained, "....and Peter was brilliant, I'm really grateful to him," she smiled brightly at the successful puncture repairer. Louise was astonished at this turn of events; realising Peter had more about him than that idle slob at home.

"Come on then, let's get down to Wainfleet and along to Skegness. It'll be one o'clock by the time we reach the clock tower." commanded Ben.

Peter looked exasperated. "Aren't you a pain in the arse? We'll go at our own speed," Louise glanced at the powerfully built cyclist. He'd taken control now!

Emma was still bemused.

With Peter now at the front and Ben glowering at the back, the group passed by Bateman's Brewery and cycled along the main road into Skegness. The clock tower showed 1.20. Ben groaned quietly. His speedometer showed 47 miles, still more than half the challenge to do.

They took lunch in a quiet café on the High Street. Peter thought how deserted the town looked out of season, with just a few pensioners walking slowly by.

Louise jumped up from her seat "Who's for a paddle, we've made the coast and we ought to celebrate!"

"I'll join you," chimed in Emma. The two men, however, refused and stayed in the café.

As the tide was out it was a long way to the water. When they got there the North Sea was cold, but it didn't matter. As the two women splashed in the water, Emma asked Louise why she had taken on the Challenge.

"Do you really want to know?" Emma nodded in response, and Louise started to explain all about Geoff.

"Aren't some men boring. You ought to tell him to get lost," Emma suggested, when Louise had finished.

Then she added encouragingly "I'll do all I can to help you finish."

"That's kind," Louise responded. " I should have left him years ago. Now tell me about you?"

Louise listened with sadness as Emma explained all about the accident. Then she looked her in the eyes, trying to ignore the deep scar across the left cheek.

"You're a very good looking girl. I can see you fancy Ben. I'm sure if you stick at it he'll come round. I hope you can make him more pleasant to us all, because I don't think I can take his rudeness much longer."

Emma smiled. Ever since she'd seen the article and Ben's picture in the paper she'd wanted to go out with him. She thought what he was trying to do for Charlie was terrific. Unfortunately this morning hadn't quite turned out as she hoped, but bolstered by Louise's encouragement, she decided to have another try.

They heard the clock tower strike two in the distance and made their way back to the Promenade, where Ben and Peter were waiting for them. Ben had wanted to cycle off and leave them but Peter had managed to persuade him that they could get back to Lincoln before dark. Even so Ben showed his anger at the two women by cycling off as soon as they arrived.

They left Skegness on the same road they had come in on, this time staying on it through Wainfleet, and not turning off until the signs for Friskney. As they started on country lanes again, Ben decided enough was enough and started to increase the pace. Louise was really starting to struggle and Emma and Peter were tiring.

Soon Ben was out of sight. The other three stopped for a drink, as the sun was quite warm now. Peter told a couple of jokes that made the others laugh and Louise received an unexpected wolf whistle from him as she bent over to tie her shoelaces, which she laughed at.

They started cycling again and heard a train in the distance. Its diesel engine became louder and it came quite close to them. The noise was quite deafening, as it thudded powerfully by on the track, just behind the hedgerows to their left.

They cycled round a tight right hand bend, and there, a hundred yards in front of them, was a terrible sight. Lying motionless on the road, across the other side of the railway track, was Ben. His cycle was some distance away from him.

"Oh God," screamed Emma "has the train hit him?"

Cycling as fast as they could, they reached Ben. They got off their cycles quickly and looked at Ben. He appeared to be unconscious. Louise examined him, expertly thought the other two. For a few seconds Ben did not move. Then to their considerable relief he opened his eyes. He looked up at the three people above him, surprised that they were standing there.

"What happened?" asked Peter.

Ben spoke falteringly. He'd had to stop and answer his mobile phone. To make up time he'd been sprint cycling. He hadn't seen the railway line. His wheels had caught in the metal. He'd been thrown over the top of his bike, clear of the track. The train thundered past, just missing him. Then he had blacked out. Ben started to try and get up. Louise gently pressed him back down.

"I think we ought to have a good look at you," she ordered.

Louise looked at the large number of cuts and grazes on his arms and legs; they'd have to be sorted before they could go on. To Emma's amazement, Louise took a full first aid kit out of her saddlebag and started gently dabbing the cuts with TCP. Emma offered to assist.

"You're not a nurse by any chance are you?" Emma asked.

Louise examined a deep gash on Ben's left arm, "How did you guess!"

Emma tenderly bathed a long cut on Ben's muscular right thigh. He faintly smiled at her. Emma looked into his deep blue eyes and smiled back.

Meanwhile Peter had set to work with his tools on Ben's cycle, adjusting wheels, straightening handlebars and replacing spokes. To a mechanic like him, repairing cars and cycles was all the same. Eventually Ben got gingerly to his feet.

"There you are Lance Armstrong, one bike as good as new," pronounced Peter handing over the cycle. Ben took it gratefully from him, and then grimaced as he got back on the seat.

"Are you OK Ben?" asked a concerned Emma.

Ben nodded in response. "Thanks for fixing my injuries." Both looked down at his long athletic legs, now covered with plasters.

"We ARE going to finish this Challenge, come what may. You're going to get the sponsorship money," said Emma, with a determination that surprised even her. Ben looked at her in appreciation.

The four cyclists, now riding together, made slow progress through Stickney and New Bolingbroke. It was clouding over, and just as they were reaching Coningsby the heavens opened, thoroughly drenching them before they could reach the "Lea Gate."

It was a bedraggled bunch that entered the pub. Louise's mascara had run all down her face and water dripped off their clothing as they walked into the bar.

Peter spent the last of his money on a round of drinks and they all tried to dry out. They sat in the pub for twenty minutes while the worst of the rain passed over. Peter, Louise and Emma talked, but Ben was silent. He looked deep in thought, but the others just assumed he was continuing to ignore them.

Eventually Ben looked at his watch, nearly 18.00 and still a long way to go.

"Shall we move?" Ben suggested. All four cyclists wearily got to their feet but Emma winced at a sharp pain in her legs. Louise saw the agonised look on Emma's scarred face. Ben looked at Emma with genuine concern.

"Not yet, I think we need to sort this young lady out. Leave this to me." Louise helped Emma back into a seated position, and then started to gently massage her legs.

"A nurse's touch," remarked Peter.

"May as well make best use of the time," commented Ben, and he asked if Peter would come with him to the far side of the room, where nobody was sitting. Peter wasn't quite sure why Ben wanted to do this, but he was of little help to Louise, so he followed Ben.

"I've been thinking about your problem, and I think I might be able to do something about it." Ben said.

Peter looked in hope at Ben, who explained that as a trainee solicitor he'd come across one or two cases like this before. Peter admitted he'd not taken legal advice, as he couldn't afford it. Ben then explained how Peter could legally reduce his contributions by over £500 a month, and he offered to come down to court tomorrow and represent him, adding "That's if we manage to get back to Lincoln in time!"

Peter was astonished, and didn't know what to say. He looked round and saw Emma was back on her feet. A huge smile radiated from his rather dirty face as he walked back across the pub floor.

"You look like you've just won on the fruit machine," said Louise.

"Rather more than that," Peter replied, beaming. They left the pub a little drier, but still very tired. Emma was very worried about her legs, but nothing was going to stop her finishing. As Louise got back on her bike she wished her shorts had been thicker and her saddle softer. She wouldn't want to sit down for a week after today!

There were still dark clouds in the sky as they left Coningsby and it was turning colder. As they cycled towards Woodhall Spa, Peter told Louise all about his problems and how Ben had offered to help him, and what a difference the extra money would make. He'd be able to live again. He wouldn't be in Lincoln Prison tomorrow night.

"I really am pleased for you, Peter." Louise smiled affectionately.

Then as Louise was explaining all about Emma, her legs and the accident, the rain came down again.

"Poor kid," sighed Peter silently reproaching himself for being so lecherous.

"You should pick on someone your own age!" admonished Louise.

Ben and Emma were somewhat in front of the other two, chattering away, and despite the driving rain they carried on cycling.

They all reached the Bardney road; cars passing by covered the cyclists in spray, drenching them. Progress was by now very slow, even Ben was showing signs of real fatigue. They stopped together for a breather in Bardney, and then had to battle against a fierce crosswind as they travelled down to Potterhanworth Booths. Louise was nearly blown off her bike twice, and despite desperate effort she was hardly moving.

Exhausted, they were forced to stop at "The Plough." They decided to go in and slumped into the seats, with hardly the energy to speak.

Ben felt total despair. "We'll never do it. My sponsors only agreed to pay up if I did the full 100 miles. Even then I'll still be over £3,000 short." Emma gave him a sympathetic look, opened her mouth to say something, but then decided against it.

Louise looked at her three other bedraggled and tired companions. "We are not giving up now, after everything we have been through. It's a good job I came prepared." From her pocket, she produced a tube of energy tablets that she handed round to three grateful cyclists.

"Now let's have a look at those legs again, Miss," she said and turned towards Emma.

"You're not a matron are you!" joked Peter. Then as he watched Louise's expert hands soothing Emma's legs, he cheekily asked, "Can I have a massage as well please?"

"Not until we finish!" replied Louise smiling.

It was well past 9 o'clock as they left the pub and started towards Washingborough. The rain was still falling on their already sodden cycling gear. It seemed ages before they cycled along Main Street. By the time they reached the golf driving range it was starting to get quite dark. Peter looked across and up at the Cathedral which loomed high above them on the right. "Ben, remind me where the Challenge ends?"

There was a silence before a response came back.

"From where we started," said Ben.

"What!" Peter exclaimed.

Nobody spoke for a minute, but each realised they'd have to tackle the awesome climb up Lindum Hill before they could finish.

As they came to the junction with Canwick Hill, Ben's cycle computer showed 98.96 miles. The final mile was going to be the hardest of all!

The slight climb up Pelham Bridge strained tired muscles. Louise wondered what on earth the big hill was going to be like. She was determined to make it though and tell her whinging husband, who would be waiting at the top of the hill, what she had achieved.He probably wouldn't care.

After the end of the Silver Street junction, it started to get harder to maintain the pace. Soon all four were out of their cycle seats.

Emma's legs were aching terribly, and Louise could hardly breathe, but they kept going. The rain continued to fall and the headlights of the oncoming cars dazzled them. Peter felt his head spinning, and Ben had a sharp pain in his side, but they struggled on.

Louise felt she couldn't go on any more and thought about stopping, then she realised what she had achieved during the last 99 miles. Nothing was going to stop her now. With steely determination she pressed hard down on the pedals again and kept going.

Emma became frightened as she heard the powerful noise of the engine of a bus, which became louder as the vehicle came closer to them. Her heart pounded. All her fears returned.She was going to be struck again. Emma tried to get as close to the kerb as possible to avoid the dangerous double- decker, now right behind her. Suddenly her front wheel caught a drain. Emma swayed towards the vehicle, on a collision course. The bus was at her side. She wobbled precariously. From behind Ben watched in horror, powerless to do anything. Was the challenge going to end in disaster?

At the last moment, out of the corner of his eye, the driver of the bus saw Emma and swerved. At the same time Emma restored her balance. An accident was averted. Emma felt numb. She had to stop.

"Come on Emma, you can do it! Keep going!" yelled Ben in encouragement.

Emma couldn't believe what she had heard, but it was just what she needed. She gripped the handlebars tightly and pedalled hard. Painfully slowly, they reached the bend at the top of the hill. Sweat was now pouring down Peter's face. Louise was in agony. Pushing with all their might into the pedals they passed under the Roman arch. The top of the hill was within sight.

"We can do it!" shouted Peter and they ground out the last 50 yards to the top of the hill.

"We've done it!" Ben let out a loud cheer, which the others joined in.

They raced down Eastgate like demented children whooping and singing, totally ignoring the puzzled stares of all those they passed.

As they turned left into the cobbles of Bailgate, Ben, Emma and Peter cycled as fast as they dared towards the Cathedral. Louise looked back up Bailgate to where cars were parked, but she didn't see any she recognised. After a brief, but poignant pause and a deep breath, she too started cycling over the cobbles.

The Cathedral was basked in a bright array of shining light. On the steps there was quite a crowd of people. Emma recognised lots of her friends, Ben could pick out many of his sponsors, including the editor. Louise looked in the crowd for Geoff, in a faint hope. She recognised nobody. He couldn't even be bothered to come to see her finish, the selfish slob.

Laying their cycles down against the Cathedral steps, Ben turned to hug the nearest person, it was Peter! Immediately Emma and Louise joined them in the embrace. They hugged as a group as cameras flashed. Then they broke into individual embraces. Peter and Emma, and Ben and Louise.

"Well done lass, after all you have been through" Peter congratulated Emma hugging her affectionately. Emma was ecstatic. "I did it! I did it!"

She looked gratefully at Peter. "Thanks so much for fixing my bike, you're a kind man," and gave him a big kiss on his cheek.Louise looked with amazement at the two of them.

"Who'd have thought it?" she said to Ben as he hugged her. She looked hopefully into his eyes. "I need you to help me, please as a solicitor," she whispered. "I'd like some advice on getting a divorce."

"Of course, give me a ring, and I'll see what I can do," Ben replied. "Well done today, you should be very proud that you made it." He paused "Thanks for patching me up as well."

"I am proud, I never believed it possible," replied Louise, "and my husband not coming to see me finish has made me realise what I've been wasting my life on." She kissed Ben.

Emma and Louise hugged each other tightly while the men shook hands.

"You kept me going, when I thought I'd was never going to make it," admitted Emma.

"Rubbish, you're a tough young woman," replied Louise. "Anyway you helped me come to a big decision in my life."

Emma smiled. "Good for you," she said.

"Now go and give Ben a big hug," ordered Louise.

The two men grinned as they watched the women. Peter looked relieved. "Thanks Ben, you've been really helpful today,".

"Let's get tomorrow sorted for you first," Ben responded, "and thanks for repairing the bike." Then he was distracted by Emma putting her arms around him.

"You did it!" she shouted and hugged him.

"Thanks, it's brilliant with all the sponsors here," and he smiled broadly. "Now only another £3,000 to go" Ben added, his smile disappearing momentarily.

"Mmmm, I think I know someone who wants to sponsor you at £30 a mile." Emma said.

Ben looked doubtful. "Who?"

"Me!" responded Emma.

"How on earth can you do that?" queried Ben.

Emma explained. "From my compensation. I got a large sum, and I'd like to use some of it for Charlie."

"Are you sure?" asked Ben, astonished.

"Never been more certain," confirmed Emma.

The editor stood close by, noting this all down. This was going to be great copy!

Ben held Emma tightly, and a tear started to roll down his cheek. All their friends were now crowding around them wanting to add their congratulations. Peter and Louise suddenly felt alone, so they started to make their way back out of the cathedral precincts.

"Can I give you a lift in my car, with your bike." Peter asked. "To your place?" Louise didn't respond.

"Or mine?" Peter suggested. "I've got a bottle of something we could share." This time Louise nodded.Peter suddenly remembered something Louise had said earlier.

"Hey, you promised me a massage if I finished," he stated.

"I'm not so sure about that," replied Louise. Then she smiled broadly. "Mind you, 100 miles is a long way!"

If Only The Window Had Opened?
By   Marjory Grierson

I should have had some portent about forthcoming events in the way that particular day had started years ago. First the milk went sour. Then notification from the hospital to say my appointment had been cancelled - yet again. But the main reason I remembered the day was because my bedroom window refused to open. I feel that is how it all started.

During this past fortnight, I received a call from my old friend Betty who still lives in my home city of Lincoln. She said she had very recently seen someone there from my past. She thought she had better let me know that he was back in England, in case on a visit home, I came face to face with him unprepared. It was Greg. Thoughtful Betty. But it did give me a jolt.

After I'd hung up, my thoughts travelled back to my early twenties, when I was almost engaged to Greg Sommerville. We had gone everywhere together, virtually inseparable. We had the same taste in music, films, literature, or so it seemed. He had proposed and eventually suggested I meet his parents. My parents were dead, so Aunty Nance had dutifully brought me up, with the minimum of fuss. Kind I suppose, but there were the occasional hints that I would stand on my own feet one day wouldn't I? Aunty was my Father's sister, who had been widowed early, childless, but fiercely determined in doing her family duty by me as she saw it.

Aunty said I would never marry him. What she really meant was, I would never be allowed to marry him. They lived in some style, several cars, frequent holidays abroad, all that sort of thing, and he was an only son. I was just a typist in the Lincoln City Council Offices. Not exactly the ideal catch. I was not even beautiful. I just didn't want to believe Aunty's pessimistic opinions.

Well I did eventually go to his home. His mother treated me coolly, her manner just about polite though distant. She could see her smitten son was anxious that I make the 'right' impression upon her. She obviously held sway in that family. I could see she was an ambitious woman and certainly a social climber. His father appeared to be a rather vague character, but friendly. I suppose my introduction was not important enough for him to be bothered with his son's 'little girl friend'.

On one tense occasion having been invited to Greg's home, by an unfortunate chance his mother and I were left alone. She told me in the arch manner such women have of imparting information to the socially inferior, her aspirations for her son. Obviously to protect her precious son from any disadvantageous influences, she mentioned he would inherit considerable money and the possibility of some social advantage by way of an elderly relative's having no family. Thereby after his father's day, he was in line for this 'social uplift' as it were. I then realised she had engineered the visit, and intended that we should be on our own. It was in order to point out how fruitless it was of me to expect to go on seeing her son, as it could not possibly lead anywhere. I was obviously persona non grata in her eyes, and definitely not in the right social category. She was clever though, for when she spoke she smiled sweetly all the time, using a soft voice, which hardly veiled the disdain for the person I was: a nobody.

I could hardly contain my composure. I felt she was not only a patronising bitch, but a loathsome snob as well. I had no answer then to this kind of approach; I felt completely out of my depth, crushed that I could be so unfairly treated by Greg's mother.

One thing Aunty Nance had taught me, and that was good manners. What I had experienced with no possible escape was humiliating. I wanted to leave at once. However I swallowed my pride and sat it out. I needed to see Greg before I left, and in any case he was running me home in his car. How could I tell him of what his mother had implied. Was love blind in his case I wondered? Greg loved me, he told me so often enough. Never once did my working girl life-style seem to be of any consequence to him. He even managed to get sceptical Aunty Nance to speak a little warmly of him. His was a sunny personality and I adored him.

Things ran on happily for a while after that, then the next thing I knew Greg was going on an extended visit to relatives in Australia. It seemed rather a rushed affair and the trumped up excuse for leaving England was to further his Father's business interests. He did have the grace to look uncomfortable when he told me about his trip.

Later on he was busy for a day or two before his departure and said he would call me to talk as he had something important to say. I had to accept it. He did call me later, and my enquiries as to his likely length of stay were given ambiguous answers, I sensed his mother was present in the room.

I felt ill at ease because although we were not actually engaged, I was assured that it would come about in the fullness of time. Had I been living on promises? I waited for three days and still no call at the house to see me or even a telephone call, after all as he knew my movements I was mystified and consequently unsure of what was going on. It would be no use ringing his house; I'd only be fobbed off.

Much later on that third day in my bedroom, I went to close the curtains as it was getting dusk. Glancing out I saw his car coming up the road, and then stop. I could just see Greg's outline sitting inside looking intently at our house as though considering should he come in. I was so excited and happy. I thought 'he's come to see me at last!' I tried to open the window. The wretched thing was stuck! I could not budge it. The carpenter Aunty called must have forgotten it and I'd not reminded her either. I was desperate now to attract Greg's attention. I kept banging on the window, and shouting 'I'm here, I'm here', but to my dismay I saw the car moving slowly away into the enveloping darkness of the late winter night. He just drove on. I was mortified.

He did not get in touch before he went. Through the bitter pain of realisation, I came to regard him as callous, and spineless, to be so much under the thumb of his parents, Mother in particular. He did write from Australia eventually and as time went on letters became fewer and no talk of returning. Then they stopped altogether. I hated myself for having been so gullible. I grieved for quite a while after, and then decided not to have any more unproductive pangs about former times and get on with my life. Perhaps after all there was too much at stake for him to go against parental pressures and just stay in his established comfort zone. That was my way of dealing with it, and trying to understand his situation.

All that was 28 years ago now. In the fullness of time, Aunty Nance left her house to me and I kept it on not only because I had been brought up there, but it's where most of my free weekends are spent. Aunty had proved to be a wise old bird. I can visit the old friends like Betty, that are still left in Lincoln with some privacy where I am known and have roots. I live in London these days, as that is my main work base. Then I got Betty's call. It did make me stop and think of long ago. One thing I was certain of, I had not thought of Greg in all that time.

I was a different person now, and busy in a very satisfying and rewarding career. What if I did meet him face to face, I knew I could cope with it. I did wonder in passing though, what had brought him back to England at this particular time. His father's firm had been in trouble about three years after he'd gone to Australia during an engineering recession, and eventually went bankrupt. Headline news in the *Lincoln Echo* but no mention of Greg having come home, even when his Father died of a heart attack soon after the firm's demise, to attend the funeral. As for his mother, I'd heard she'd moved away.

Aunty Nance mellowed with time and lived into her eighties long enough to see me become successful, and achieve my focus in life to excel in my profession. Being Aunty, she took the credit for helping me get on. She was proud of my achievements and I was grateful for her support. I became the daughter she never had. She was always glad I had been jilted, and a bit smug about it. 'Saw it coming' She said. She chuckled when she said it too. Not one to pull her punches my Aunty Nance. I came to love and understand her, and I missed her dreadfully after she died.

I loved being in the Welfare Department of the City Council where I had worked when I knew Greg, and although then I was only typing the reports of children who needed help, I was determined to learn more especially after he had gone. At first to fill the void in my life and afterwards, because I genuinely wanted to be of greater use. I had done well at school but hadn't considered I could go further.

After some time spent at night school I qualified enough to gain entrance to a University. That was when

Aunty Nance told me about her 'nest egg'. "Couldn't tell you before" she said, "You were too wound up with that Greg business". 'Now you can do what you ought to do'. She was right. She'd been saving up all those years, she'd always believed I could do more than just be a typist. 'Judith Durrance,' she had said, "I don't want my money wasted, so get on with it".

Several years later, by one of those quirks of fate when I had become quite well-known for my welfare work, I was invited to open a retirement home for the elderly poor and disadvantaged in Lincolnshire. As I had had a great deal of international experience in many different social areas, I was asked to give my opinion on any improvement that the local authority could incorporate. To that end I was given a guided tour around the modern and friendly home.

Whilst sitting in one of the communal rooms having a cup of tea provided by one of the lady residents, I was aware of the feeling that I was being observed very closely by an elderly lady in the room. I turned towards her, and with a start, realised she looked so like Greg's Mother but much older. Eventually, as I went around the room I could see that it was indeed his mother. She was still quite upright and thin, but the old arrogance had gone, in fact she seemed somehow vulnerable and out of place. I was about to be introduced to her by the Home's head warden, when she interrupted and spoke to me. "I know this lady" she said. To hear me being called a 'lady' from her lips was a real surprise. For a moment I was caught off guard remembering our last encounter. I wondered what she was going to say, as she had been known in the past as one not to hold back or mince her words. However in this situation I suddenly realised that unbelievably I was the one with all the advantages, and - the guest of honour.

After she had overcome her surprise the Head Warden suggested that I might like to have a moment with Mrs Sommerville, and continue with the tour in five minutes, reminding me that my assistant had indicated my schedule was tight. I sat down by Mrs Sommerville, not knowing what to expect.

"How are you Mrs Sommerville?" I began. She looked at me with a wry little smile, "bearing up under the circumstances," she said with an air of acceptance of her obviously changed lifestyle. "You seem to have done well for yourself," she said next. "But I can see now, how badly I underestimated you all those years ago. By all accounts you are not only highly respected in your profession, but a woman of some consequence."

Although this woman had altered the course of my life, I could not flaunt the advantage of my current status as she obviously saw it. So I put my hand on hers, and as she did not flinch, I said. "I was sorry to hear of Mr. Sommerville's death."

"It was sudden, and his affairs were so complicated," she said with a sigh. She paused. Then went on. "Greg married you know, but I only saw him once sometime after his father had died."

That did shock me. It must have been years since that event. In spite of myself I said, "Do you mean to tell me that he does not communicate with you at all?"

"No," she said resignedly.

I was at a loss for words with this woman, who had once seriously implied that I was not good enough for her precious son. "He stayed in Australia and never came home again."

How could I not feel sorry for her now, old, probably lonely and because of where she now lived, without adequate means.

At that moment the Head Warden gently reminded me that my official car was waiting at the door to take me to my next appointment. I got up ready to say my farewells, when I heard my name. "Judith!" I bent down and looked Greg's Mother fully in the face, then held out my hand.

She took it and held on to it, "I wish..." she stumbled over the next words, "Things could have been different..."

It was her starchy little way of acknowledging having treated me in the past unkindly to say the least. As I appeared to her on that day, it must have been galling to find I had made my own considerable mark in the world, and without her son. I never saw her again as she died the year following my visit.

I found the message on my home answering service a week ago. I recognised the voice at once. He will ring again soon it said, hoping I will be in. Greg rang a few days later at the weekend in the evening, and sounded just like he did years ago. He had come to England because his son was entering university in Lincoln, and he wanted to make sure he had somewhere decent to live. During a long conversation he filled me in on his life to the present time. I just listened with the appropriate 'reallys', 'ums' and 'ahs'. It was obvious he just wanted to talk. I wondered why after all these years with no contact.

He said he was now a widower after 27 years of marriage. Eventually he tentatively asked had I married? On hearing I had not, asked what were the chances of a meeting for old time's sake. He said he was speaking from a London hotel but could come up to Lincoln during the following week if that would be convenient. I was relieved to find I felt not one pang of heartache, I had really grown away from the naïve girl I was when we first met. Would it be the same if I actually saw him?

I know I had improved, quite considerably. The photos told their own story. I dressed well, had a good hairdresser and was now a poised and self-assured woman. My job required it. I was well-travelled and had a very interesting and fulfilling lifestyle. I also had the confidence of my peers in the job. I told him that I worked most of the time in London and we could meet somewhere there. He seemed delighted at this prospect and asked where. I mentioned that I worked in the Palace of Westminster and had he ever had a 'visitor' tour round there? He said no, but sounded intrigued, and asked 'was I some big wig's secretary there now'? I was vague about what I actually did, but said I was a small cog in a very large wheel. This he readily accepted, and to my amusement, remarked that in such a large place it was inevitable.

I offered to get him a private guided tour as a guest if he would like it. He was pleased at this, and assumed that guiding people around Westminster was now my full time job. I said I would arrange for an usher to meet him just inside the building where he would be vetted by the police. He was to ask for me by name. Normal procedure these days. Once this routine had been gone through he would be taken to the office I worked in. We could then take it from there.

On the appointed day I waited in expectation of how Greg would find me after all these years. Whilst waiting for him to arrive, I mused how yet another quirk of fate, had once made a certain window stay firmly shut and wondered if it would have made a difference anyway!

From my office I could see the corridor alongside the outer office and from this vantage point, saw Greg sometime before he saw me. He looked almost the same, older of course and tanned, his greying hair still plentiful.

His face was careworn, however, he appeared not to have put on any noticeable weight.

The usher admitted him to the outer office and I heard my Private Secretary say, "If you will come this way please Sir, Baroness Durrance is free to see you now!"

Jump for Freedom by   Julia Peach

Even in an aircraft two thousand feet above the ground Martha's high pitched voice continued to scream through my head.

"Bob, you will give yourself a heart attack. Bob, you are too old. Oh Robert, you are so pathetic."

I had hoped that up here I could get away from the missus, concentrate on my jump and enjoy the freedom I would have amongst the clouds. Martha and I have been married for forty years. Whilst we were courting she was the woman of my dreams, but as soon as that gold band was placed upon her finger she changed. The pilot's voice interrupted my thoughts.

"Not much longer mate. Better start getting yourself prepared. Fred will give you a hand."

I had to tell Martha about the parachute jump right at the very start. I couldn't keep secrets but even if I had tried she would have found out. She was like that. She was devious and cunning, very controlling and often cruel. The first time I told her she went off into a rage and my life was made miserable for days.

I was determined this time though. I wanted to complete this jump for myself. To prove that I was still a man and not some weak wimp that was manipulated by a woman. To solve the problem of her constant nagging I had even gone out and invested in some ear plugs. Every time she droned on about the jump I would discreetly pop them in place. They worked a treat as her nagging just became a muted mutter. Luckily Martha was none the wiser. I think she just assumed that I was ignoring her. In hindsight I should have bought ear plugs many years earlier.

I pulled my black tee shirt over my head and placed it

on the floor along with my jacket and trousers. Although Martha was aware of the jump, the finer, more delicate details, had only been discussed with John the pilot, Fred and myself.

Fred came over to help me fasten my helmet.

"Are you sure you want to go ahead with this Bob?"

I smiled.

"Oh yea. I can't wait to see the old bat's face when she realizes I've succeeded with this." I looked down proudly at my body. The finer, more delicate, details were now obvious. I was only wearing a helmet, the parachute pack, some socks, black boots and a black Calvin Klein thong.

"What do you think Fred? I'm not in bad shape for a seventy-one year old am I?"

To prepare for this jump I had become a member of our local gym. I had even paid out a small fortune for a personal trainer. It was hard at first but at a steady pace I soon toned up. Martha saw the difference and used it to her advantage. The sexual activities I had escaped for years were now unavoidable. Martha loved a good romp and now I had no excuse. For those occasions my imagination was stretched to its limits as Martha became a glamorous film star. It always worked so long as my eyes were kept shut and my ear plugs were firmly in place.

"Two thousand five hundred feet. Are you ready?" The pilot's voice came over the speaker. I could feel my heart pounding. This was the moment I had trained for.
I was so excited.

"Yea. I'm ready Boss. Let's open that door."

I had completed six hours of ground training but had never before jumped from a plane. This was going to be a totally new experience.

With the door open I peered out. For miles I could see little islands of cotton wool ball clouds floating amongst the baby blue sky. The scene was magnificent and after inhaling the fresh, unpolluted air I felt ready to be part of it. I stepped out of the plane. Within seconds the two way mandatory radio crackled into existence.

"You're doing okay Bob" Reassured the pilot.

"Yes……I'm fine." I shouted against the buffeting wind "See you on the ground." I tried to sound confident, but now as I was free falling from the sky I began to wonder if my confidence had reached the ground before me.

"Right, I am releasing the static line, remember the canopy will open when you are exposed to some air flow." The pilot's instructions were clear but unforeseen circumstances prevented me from answering. The pilot had mentioned air flow but this I had already become intimately familiar with.

"Shit…..Blimey….Bloody hell." I was cursing under my breath. My parachute had opened jolting me into an upright position but my thong had become like a hungry snake, constricting and suffocating my privates. I reached down trying to release them, but every time I gave them some slack the air flow pushed upwards again, squeezing and twisting them further.

"Damn." I muttered again. No matter how hard I tried,"Operation Please Release Me" remained unsuccessful. I knew I would have to give up and suffer the torture.

I had promised myself before the jump that I wouldn't look down. Acrophobia was just another of my weaknesses and one which Martha constantly used to taunt me. She seemed to have a mission in life to make me seem inadequate amongst her rapidly declining circle of friends.

"You are about one thousand five hundred feet. Have you had a good look down at the view yet?" The pilot's voice interrupted my thoughts. It was as if he had read my mind.

"No, but......." I replied. I had already taken a good look but the view had stopped at my tangled thong. I had been too preoccupied to look any further. The radio crackled again but I couldn't hear what was being said. Martha's voice had intruded, once again, into my head and taken over.

"Bob, you know you can't do this....Robert, for goodness sake admit to your inadequacies .... Robert, you can't even climb onto the first rung of a step ladder ...." She was always exaggerating and, although I do admit to having a fear of heights, she always made it out to be one thousand times worse. Her friends, most of whom were devoted church goers, eventually saw through her pretence and gave up on the friendship. She blamed me of course stating that I had pushed them away. I didn't argue but I was silently glad that the majority had finally discovered the truth. I just wished it was as easy for me to leave her.

"Bob can you hear me?"

"Yes...Sorry mate." I had forgotten about the radio and my concentration had lapsed.

"I was saying have you had a good look down at the view yet?"

I wanted to look further than the tops of my legs and now seemed to be the right time to do it.

"I'm about to look now Boss." I replied.

I inhaled deeply trying to steady my nerves before glancing at the scene that was literally unfolding beneath me.

"Fuck!" I wasn't usually one to say such an awful profane word but a sudden excruciating pain had forced me into using it. I looked down to the cause of the problem and was both stunned and shocked with what I saw. My thong this time had disappeared into my groin. All I could see were my bits being violently tossed and swung around with the force of the air.

Now I wanted to turn back time. I wanted to start again or perhaps not start at all. This was a disaster and I hadn't even reached the ground yet. I tried again to manoeuvre my thong into a dignified position. I tugged even harder now but it was determined to remain firmly super glued into the crevice. I glanced down briefly at the ground. It was looming up fast. I knew I needed to do something quickly if was going to land with some modesty. I pulled at them again mustering some extra strength. This time it worked. I couldn't have been more relieved as finally my precious cargo was under wraps.

"You are about One hundred and fifty feet from the landing field."

"Okay" I shouted back. I was okay now. It was wonderful to finally be in control. All I had to do now was concentrate on a perfect landing.

"Good luck mate. See you on the ground."

Suddenly another disaster struck.

"Please no." I muttered pleadingly as I watched my thong flutter teasingly beyond my reach. The abused stitching had conked out and now I had to think of a contingency plan fast. The obvious, if not the only one, was land, unhitch, run and hide.

Whilst I was hunting for a hiding place I noticed something else. I thought it was a figment of my imagination at first, but after taking a second glance the horror of the situation materialised.

"Oh no, why is this happening to me." I couldn't believe it. After every thing I had just gone through something even worse was about to happen.

Now as I got closer I recognised Martha standing on the ground. She was the bulky, short one standing amongst a large group of her ex-friends and acquaintances. I couldn't believe she had bought them along to watch. This was a private jump. I had only told the old witch as her beady eyes surveyed everything. There was some reason that she was down there. She had planned and plotted something but I just couldn't fathom it out.

"No.......Oh hell." It occurred to me then. I had told Martha everything but had deliberately and for obvious reasons excluded the thong. Martha was as much in the dark about that as I was about the audience she had raked together.

Martha didn't come home that night but our local paper explained it all. The headlines read *Local people shocked as naked pensioner jumps from the skies*. A photo had been plastered underneath. I was relieved to discover that an X had been stamped over the evidence. The article stated that Martha's idea had been brilliant and that over one thousand pounds had been raised for charity. The phone rang the following day.

"Robert you are a complete bloody self centred fool. I want a divorce now"

"Yes dear." I replied, as a huge uncontrollable smile spread across my face.

After forty years, more than a life sentence I was finally free. I had planned this jump for myself, for my own peace of mind. I had never even contemplated that it would become a jump for freedom.

Fatal Love   by   Julia Peach

I had seen him almost immediately he had entered the lounge. He was tall with ashen blonde hair and on a closer inspection I noticed that he had penetrating glacial blue eyes. I was instantly attracted to him. Now all I had to do was get him to notice me and hope that he would feel the same.

I took a few deep breaths whilst smoothing down my skirt. I needed to slow down my heart rate and be in control for when I made my move.

In the past I had never had much luck with men. Usually the ones I found were already seriously involved and with two or three kids.

"Diane darling, I am so glad you made it." Michelle's high pitched squeaky voice interrupted my hypnotic trance. We had known each other since secondary school and gradually over the years we had become good friends.

Michelle loves parties and in the past has been the host to many excellent ones.

Tonight's rave was obviously going to be no exception. She had spent a fortune on spooky paraphernalia and candles and had managed to create the perfect ambience for an eerie Halloween party.

"Well you know me. I'm always on husband patrol so I couldn't miss this opportunity." I replied.

As it was the 31ˢᵗ October the guests needed to be in a spooky fancy dress. As usual Michelle had gone to town. Her costume was as spectacular as ever. She was dressed as a glamorous witch. The usual green face, hooked nose and warts were deliberately excluded. It was typical of Michelle to apply her make-up to enhance her looks not penalise them. Her dress was ankle length and sleeveless and had been cut into a perfect shape to show off her size twelve figure and her augmented 32 double E boobs. She was a dressmaker by trade and I am sure that most of her parties were fancy dress so that she could show off her fabulous creations.

I had randomly scraped my costume together this afternoon. It was never worth making a huge effort at these parties as Michelle was always the belle of the ball. I had borrowed a gothic style skirt and blouse from my neighbour. Then just bought the odd accessory and a vampiric face painting kit to finish the look. The cheap plastic fangs were my only problem. They finished the look to perfection but despite how hard I tried I developed a lisp and spluttered whenever I tried to talk. I discovered that early on and now they were firmly tucked away in my pocket.

"Well do enjoy yourself sweetie." Michelle giggled. "And good luck with the men."

As Michelle walked away I turned back, longingly looking for the blonde stranger but mysteriously he had vanished.

I saw him later standing alone in the kitchen. The room heaved with guests so it was easy to make myself inconspicuous. I wanted to spy on the stranger and psych out my prey before going in for the kill. My newly adopted behaviour stemmed from all the wildlife programmes that had been shown on the Discovery channel just lately. In some ways it made me feel like a lioness out stalking but if it improved my man hunting skills I felt anything was worth a try.

Billy and Charlotte were among the guests in the kitchen. They were Michelle's neighbours and had become good friends of mine over the years. They knew only too well that I longed for a man and a stable relationship. At a dinner party last year they had named me 'Desperate Di ' and the name had stuck.

I edged back into the gap between the door and the wall. If Billy and Charlotte saw me I knew they would instantly come over to say hello.

The stranger was wearing a smoking jacket, scarlet cravat and dark slacks. His anachronistic dress sense reminded me of a gentleman from the early part of the 20th century. If he was portraying himself as a spook he had me totally baffled.

I stifled a giggle as it suddenly occurred to me that he could be at the wrong party. Last year that had happened to me. I turned up as a tart to a medieval banquet. My black, bum hugging mini skirt and my almost see through skimpy top caused me total embarrassment. I had even worn a 32 B bra. I was told that it would uplift my boobs. It was far too small. Consequently I had two large mammary glands bulging over the edges.

"Edward! I've been looking for you everywhere." Michelle was in the kitchen now grabbing his hand. "Come on let's dance. A slow song is playing at the moment."

I gritted my teeth. Once again I had left it too late. My prey had been snatched from under my nose. Desperate for some fresh air to clear my head I stepped out into the garden.

I knew I had drunk too much. I felt slightly dizzy and

it was becoming increasingly hard to focus. I stepped on the line between the paving slabs and tried to follow their path. In just two steps I felt myself stagger. I tried to right myself but I was too late. I stumbled side ways and fell against a large apple tree.

"Shit." I muttered angrily to myself.

Normally I was a placid person preferring to take a back seat rather than diving in and causing upheaval. Michelle probably didn't even know what she was doing but this time she had really rattled my cage. The more I stood here the more determined I became to fight back.

My last boyfriend could have been an ideal husband. He was deliciously handsome with a great personality. We had been going out together for a whole year, two days and eight hours. I was ready to accept his proposal. Eventually he broke it off and the reason completely shocked me. I can remember all the text messages. He used to contact me to explain that he had to work late. Only at the very end did I realize that those messages were total lies. They should have been interpreted as 'sorry but I have promised Matthew some rampant anal sex.' It was just my sort of luck to pick a bloke that was in the process of changing sides.

Michelle was still playing the field. I knew she would just have Edward for a couple of nights to satisfy her sexual desires. If she had an opportunity to seduce him she wouldn't hesitate. She would grab it with both hands. The alcohol and the reminiscing made my head feel as if it was about to explode. I was ready now to salvage my disastrous evening.

"Fancy a change of partner?" I had marched non-stop from the garden. Now I was barging in separating Michelle and Edward from their cosy smooch.

"Of course. How could I refuse such a beautiful

lady." Edward replied. "Please excuse me Michelle."

I was glad of the compliment but desperately had to disguise my snigger. My freaky make-up made me look anything but beautiful.

He released his hand from Michelle's and took hold of mine. "My name is Edward Follingsworth."

"I know." I replied. "I'm Diane."

We danced for ages. Edward seemed to glide across the floor with me enfolded within his arms. Eventually the music stopped and the disc jockey announced that he was going to take a five minute break.

"Let's get a drink. I don't know about you but I'm gasping." I didn't want to let go of Edward's hand. I was concerned that if I did Michelle would steal him away again.

"Off course. Shall we adjourn to the kitchen?" he replied.

His mannerisms, his skilled dancing and his speech were so unlike any man I have ever come across. I was intrigued to find out a bit more, sipping on a glass of chilled Chardonnay I felt ready to ask him some questions.

"So Edward who taught you to dance like that?"

"Many years of experience darling." he replied.

I took another sip of my wine.

"Have you been to any of Michelle's other parties?" I asked.

"No." Edward shook his head.

"You have a lovely accent. Where are you from?" I tried again. He was obviously listening as his eyes keenly focused on mine.

"From overseas." came his reply.

The music began to play again in the other room and Edward took my hand.

"Shall we dance?" He asked.

I know men are generally not great conversationalists but somehow I couldn't help feeling that Edward was holding something back. Like earlier his hand was cold. Unusually cold considering the house was very warm. Once again I chose to ignore it. If I commented about it I knew I would only get a half hearted answer. I thought of the phrase, cold hands, warm heart and I focused my attention on that.

Eventually after another hour of continuous dancing my feet began to object. I was wearing a pair of new shoes and their leather had begun digging ferociously into my heels. I didn't want to stop but my newly formed blisters were giving me no choice.

Reluctantly I released my hands from behind Edward's neck. "Let's stop for a bit and sit down."
Edward didn't answer but as I started to move away he followed.

"You must be so fit." I removed my shoes and collapsed down onto the settee beckoning Edward to sit next to me. "Are you a member of a gym?"

I opened the top button of my blouse, shaking it to allow some air onto my skin. I was uncomfortably hot. Edward, I noticed, wasn't even sweating.

"No. I just make sure I stick to a special diet." he replied.

Edward longingly looked at my bare flesh. I waited patiently undoing two more buttons to entice him some more.

He still didn't make a move so I pulled up my skirt revealing my upper thighs. I was running out of flirtatious techniques. I didn't want to come on too strong or reveal too much in such a public place.

"Please excuse me." Edward stood up. "I'll see you later." I was dumb struck. Our relationship, sex even, was being offered here. Any man would jump at such an opportunity. I just couldn't comprehend that he had just stood up and walked away. I needed a drink. A pick-me-up to allow me to cope with yet another rejection. I was beginning to understand now why folk turn to alcohol in their darkest hours. I left the lounge and ambled into the kitchen.I was determined not to cry but a single tear was now rolling down my cheek. I retrieved a napkin from the pile and quickly wiped it away hoping that no-one would notice. A sorrowful glance or a pitying hug was the last thing I needed right now.

Suddenly a loud bang startled me and it took me a couple of seconds for it to register that it was a firework. Michelle had told me that fireworks would finish the evening but I had completely forgotten. From the kitchen window I could see a fantastic cascade of bright colours showering down from the sky. I hurried outside with the other guests to watch the display.

A missile had been launched now. It screeched as it shot upwards into the dark night. Eventually it reached its maximum height and the noise abruptly stopped. I watched as an array of shooting stars twinkled on their downward spiral.

"Diane…Thank goodness. Where have you been?"

Michelle grabbed my arm. "Please give me a hand."

She gasped. "I feel awful."

Another firework lit up the sky.

"Bloody hell. You look terrible. What on earth has happened?"

The illuminations allowed me to see her pale complexion and I couldn't help but notice the beads of sweat shining out across her forehead.

"I don't know but I think I might puke." She raised her hand up to her mouth and I heard her heave.

"Come on lets get you inside." I said placing my arm around her shoulder. We had only taken a couple of steps when I felt her slump against me. I staggered as I tried to support her body.

"Bloody typical of you girl." I muttered lowering her to the ground. "You should get an Oscar for this performance."

Billy and Charlotte were standing nearby and had seen Michelle faint. Billy removed his jacket to cover her whilst Charlotte hurried to the kitchen to fetch a glass of water. I rolled her slightly onto one side supporting her head. I had read somewhere that this 'recovery' position stopped a person choking on their tongue.

Gradually Michelle's eyes flickered open. She looked disorientated.

"It's okay. You fainted." I reassured her. "Let's sit you up a bit. Can you pull up on me?"

"I'm so tired.......need to go to sleep......where's Edward?" She was muttering but I managed to decipher a few words. I wanted to ask her why she was looking for Edward but at the last minute decided against it.

The three of us decided that the best option would be to get Michelle up to bed. It was a struggle and she fainted again on the upstairs landing. Eventually though we fulfilled our aim and she was safely tucked up in her bed. Billy told all the guests the party was over and then we set about clearing up the house.

It was a mess. Empty beer cans and wine bottles had been randomly discarded on the floor. Ashtrays were full and overflowing and empty or half full glasses had just been left everywhere. Charlotte and I began to retrieve all the glasses and place them next to the sink.

"What's wrong with her Diane?"

Charlotte's expression was solemn but the sound in

her voice revealed a genuine concern for her friend.

"I have no idea but it came on really fast. She looked radiant when I first arrived." I knew my comment held some jealous sarcasm. Luckily Charlotte didn't seem to notice.

Billy walked over to the sink and began washing the mound of glasses that we had collected.

"I've been thinking.......could someone have spiked her drink?"

I heard Charlotte take a shocked gasp. "Billy! Surely not at one of Michelle's parties."

Charlotte was very prim and proper but the down side of this was her naivety.

"He's right Charlotte. It could easily have happened. People are not always what they seem." Sometimes, and it was only occasionally, I did succeed in rational sociological summations.

"Let's just finish up here and you two go home. I'll stop overnight and see how she is in the morning. If she gets worse I'll give her doc a call." I smiled across at Charlotte hoping to reassure her.

The stillness in the house now was almost eerie. Just a couple of hours ago it had buzzed with activity and now it was deadly quiet. I yawned. I felt physically exhausted but mentally I was finding it difficult to unwind. I poured myself another glass of wine hoping it would allow me to relax.

Walking through to the lounge made me shiver. The air was unusually cold in here compared to the kitchen. I leaned up against a radiator and closed my eyes. It was soothing to feel its warmth permeate through my skirt and onto my skin.

"I know exactly what you need right now."

I jumped at the sound of a voice and spun round towards it's direction.

"Who's there?" I called out nervously. It was a masculine voice so I knew it wasn't Michelle. "What do you want?"

"I'm sorry to have unnerved you. I just wanted to see you again." A figure emerged from near the fireplace. "Please, I won't hurt you."

I recognised the voice now. "Edward!" I exclaimed. "It's you."

"And you need to calm down. Here let me pour you another."

Just looking at him was causing a tingling sensation to creep up my spine. I had never felt like this just by looking at a man before. I wondered if my feelings were symptoms of the true meaning of falling in love.

"Feeling better.?" Edward brushed his fingers along the side of my face.

"Oh yes, most definitely." I replied.
Edward's finger's proceeded to circle the outline of my lips.

"You are enjoying this. Would you like some more?" His accented words glided from his tongue.

"Off course." I managed to reply. I couldn't refuse. It didn't matter to me now that he had walked out on me earlier.I moved my face closer to his, beckoning for his lips to touch mine. I closed my eyes and waited. Edward's lips felt like ice against my own but still I encouraged him to continue. I was enjoying every second of this passionate kiss. I hoped that it would never end. Edward must have read my thoughts as it lasted for as long as I could hold my breath.

After the kiss I kept my eyes shut as his lips and tongue slowly migrated to my right ear. I felt his tongue circle the outside until it reached my lobe. Next I felt the hardness of his teeth touch my skin and gently nibble at my flesh. My tingling sensation intensified, my heart began to flutter even more and I could feel myself becoming weak at the knees.

I felt dreamy and hypnotised. Captivated under the influence of a love spell. His arms were wrapped around me now pulling me closer. I didn't resist. I couldn't resist. I wanted to go further.

Suddenly my feet had risen from the floor and I realized that he had lifted me up into his arms. There was no struggle, no huffing and puffing for breath. He picked me up as easily as I would lift a baby from its cot. Then gently and with me still in his arms he slowly lowered himself down onto the settee. I felt his lips tickle the nape of my neck. I opened my eyes briefly. His face was strangely glowing. I closed them again and without saying anything I willed him to go on.

A sharp pain in my neck caused me to jerk backwards. Edward ignoring my obvious discomfort began pulling me in closer. As the pain eased I felt a sticky, wet substance trickle down my neck.

As my energy seeped out from me I forced my eyelids open. I knew what was happening now but I felt powerless to be able to do anything about it. I looked into Edward's face. It was glowing as his grey complexion flushed with pink. I watched as his fangs slowly retracted.

I closed my eyes once more knowing that this time I would never awake.

To Have and To Hold   by   Elizabeth Selby

I knew that I was a misfit the minute that she tried me on. She had come into the shop and demanded to have a proper look at me.

I cringed behind the more elegant numbers who were on the rails beside me. Well let's face it. I just couldn't hope to compete against them! My full-length once beautiful veil lay bedraggled beneath me. The seed pearls scattered across my bodice were about to fall off. And the white petals of the Michaelmas daisy blooms were wilting.

I was lifted from the rail and the assistant looked askance at the customer.

"I want to try it on?" demanded the young woman.

The assistant obliged.

Inside the changing room the young woman stripped down to her undies, and held me up to the light.

I shrank. My crumples revealing themselves even more under the harsh strip lighting. But there was a smile on the face of the young woman.

"Wonderful – oh you are just perfect," she said.

She was talking to ME! I perked up, thoroughly elated at the kind words of the wearer, that some of the smaller creases disappeared.

"Are you alright in there?" enquired the assistant.

"Perfect thanks – I'm just fine," came the reply. And moments later, she came out of the cubicle, carrying me proudly in her arms.

"You will take it I presume?" asked the assistant somewhat facetiously.

"Of course I will. It just needs a little tender love and attention."

I wiggled with pleasure as I was folded into the large plastic bag.

"There goes a couple of misfits," whispered the assistant to her colleague.

I moved up and down in the bag. Misfits we may be, but I couldn't wait for my new life to begin. The door clanged behind us as we left the shop.

Workplace Experiences   by   Elizabeth Selby

Although I have had a variety of career changes over the years, my favourite job was as a shorthand typist back in the 1960's when I first left school.

I started work at Ruston and Hornsby, a large engineering firm in 1962, after completing my training at Lincoln Technical College on Monks Road.

My first encounter with the works was an interview with Miss Panther the personnel officer. She was a dragon, something out of the Hammer house horror film, and her name suited her perfectly. We were all in awe of her. Over the next few years she was to cross my path, and cause problems and heartbreak. But anyway, I passed her scrutiny and was offered a job in the Packing Shop as a typist. I went along to meet my new boss there, Joan Stanham. It was an instant dislike on her part at first glance!

She very unpleasantly told me, 'I expect to see you here at 7.30 tomorrow.'

I quaked in my size five and a half shoes, "Yes Ma'am," I replied reverently. The thought of catching the 6.45am bus filled me with dread and would I oversleep?

Anyway, 7.30am the next morning I was in the Packing Shop Offices ready to go. The place vibrated with machines, working.

"Okay, let's see how you fill in these forms. That's your typewriter, now get on with it." Said Joan Stanham.

She hadn't even introduced me to the other two girls in the office at that stage. I learnt over the next few days that their names were Audrey and Irene. At least though, I could show I was a competent typist. At 10am Joan told me that as I was the last in the office, so I was to be tea girl.

"There's the kettle, now off you go and don't hang about. Ask one of the men on the shop floor where to fill it."

Timidly I went out and approached one of the men, my face red with embarrassment as a chorus of whistles pierced the air, noisier than even the sounds of the engines being tested.

"Over there Miss," said one man pointing towards a tap.

I rushed over to fill my kettle, wishing to get away from the howls and catcalls that were coming from all directions. I didn't think my Royal Tartan pinafore dress and white piecrust shirt was going to create that much attention and I couldn't wait to return to my office.

"Took your time didn't you. I hope you were not chatting up the apprentices," snapped Joan.

Still blushing I replied that I hadn't and made tea. Then rather shyly I asked if I may leave the room and could I go to the toilet. Joan looked at me as though I had asked to have a holiday, and that it was impertinent to even mention that I should need to leave the office.

"Ladies toilets are over by the Main Entrance," she growled at me.

My heart flipped, they were miles away.

"We only leave the office one at a time, saves you girls from talking too much to one another." Joan added.

Audrey and Irene looked at each other, Irene smothering a snigger.

Joan glared at her, "Get on with your work," she snapped.

The girls gave me a sympathetic look.

Oh well needs must and bravely I left the office and made my way to the Ladies. Past men who howled like wolves at me, with head down I rushed up the aisles, past the noise from all the machinery, deafening. I almost ran now, eager and desperate to reach the sanctuary of the Ladies. And at last there it was ahead of me, safety!

But what a sight greeted me. There standing over one of the washbasins was a woman cleaning her false teeth. I stood watching this spectacle in horror, because she wasn't using toothpaste, instead she was using the green carbolic soap provided by the firm. Stomach churning at this dreadful sight I dived into the nearest loo, slamming the door behind me in the panic of wanting to get away from such a horrible sight.

My stomach heaved; I hope she had gone by the time I came out! But no, I was greeted by the sight of those dreaded teeth now sitting in a plastic cup with a lump of green soap beside them.

Another young girl looked at me and raised her eyebrows; "Hi you must be new, as I haven't seen you before."

I nodded, and we left the ladies with the toothy woman still looking at the glass and its contents.

"Oh that's Annie, she does that everyday, you will get use to seeing them," said the girl, who I learnt was called Dorothy, she worked in a nearby office. Glad of her company, I walked part of the way back to the Packing Shop. The wolf whistles didn't seem quite so bad when I had somebody with me. I even managed a sideways glance at one young lad in green overalls. He looked nice, I thought.

So back to typing, endless forms and reports and then it was teatime again.

"Off you go and don't stand talking to any young men," demanded Joan.

As if I would I said to myself rather rebelliously! Again I filled the kettle from the same tap. I saw one of the men watching me carefully but he said nothing.

And so began my life as a typist in the packing shop, an endless round of typing and tea making, and little chance to fraternise with my work colleagues. Joan Stanham soon stamped on that if we so much as uttered a friendly good morning to each other.

Then one day as I was doing my usual chore of filling the kettle, one of the men in blue overalls came over to me.

"Why don't you use the main tap luv?" he asked.

Askance, I told him that I was using the main tap and pointed to it.

The man chortled, "That's an engine you are draining water from!"

In horror I looked at him. What on earth had I been doing over the last few weeks? I had been making tea with stagnant water and those men had stood by and watched me! Then I thought to myself that it was a pity that I hadn't poisoned Joan, but of course if I had done that, then we would all have been poisoned.

Did I tell anyone in the office? Of course not. They say silence is golden, and no harm had been done. I was relieved when a job opportunity came up on the works notice board for a secretary to Mr Dunn in the wages Department. Like a shot I went along to Miss Panther's office and asked to apply for the post.

As usual, Miss Panther greeted me with disdain, "Why do you want to leave your present job?"

Well, I could hardly tell her that I was in danger of murdering my present boss by poisoning her with stagnant water, so I replied that I wished to improve my career prospects. She told me she would get in touch with me at a later date, and I was dismissed. With a heavy heart I went back to the Packing Shop. I knew I wouldn't get the job.

However to my delight a few days later I got a call to attend the Panther's lair again. I opened her door and went inside.

"Miss Bartram, I am please to say Mr Dunn would like you to go along and see him immediately. He has looked at your work report, and thinks you will make him a good secretary."

So began a happy association for the next seven years with one of the nicest bosses ever.

Roman Steps   by   Sharon Horne

The air inside the cathedral seemed thin, rarified, insufficient to fill the vastness. The soft sunlight giving a comfortable warm atmosphere that felt timeless, eternal. Lincoln Cathedral's majestic nave was enclosed by limestone walls with stained glass windows along both sides. Each window rich in the colour of precious jewels: ruby red, emerald green, diamond white and sapphire blue. In front of the windows tall pillars of stone and marble, arched as if joined in praying hands, above each glass montage.

"This is something else, I'm not sure where to start it's so magnificent," said Ben as he took out an information leaflet from his back pocket. It was rolled into a tube like a Savannah cigar. He rolled out the piece of paper as Mae, his traveling companion, looked around for an information desk.

"I'll see when the guided tours start, we should be able to find the Teaching window."

Mae dressed in a long denim skirt and flat open back sandals shimied across the flagstone floor, smoothly circling around awe struck tourists like Ginger Rogers on the dance floor. Ben watched as Mae almost courtseyed as she elegantly disappeared around a stone corner.

Standing alone now, he slowly became aware of slight changes all around him; he felt perplexed, something wasn't quite right. Surrounding tourists were becoming distant like actors on a small silent black and white t.v. screen. Ben stared as their outlines gently became translucent. Mystically, a choir began to sing in harmony with the deep tubular tones of the cathedral organ.

Confused and clumsy, Ben turned to face the West front of the cathedral, where he could just see the wooden doorway he had walked through earlier. It was slightly open, a shaft of daylight cutting through the haze. At least there was a way out, but this was only a small relief to Ben who was beginning to feel apprehensive like a lost child searching for a familiar face.

As he turned, a man appeared at the side entrance in the cathedral wall opposite. Ben opened his mouth to speak but could only mouth silently. This man stood proud and upright, the physical image of a fighter but not dressed in a fighting uniform. Images flashed through Ben's befuddled mind. He could see 'Gladiator' - Russell Crowe and Richard Burton as Caesar in Cleopatra. But this man was plainly dressed in simple clothing, a thick tunic and leather belt worn over a pair of cropped trousers.

Ben continued to stare in disbelief. The man was Roman and surely all Roman men were soldiers at sometime in their lives. Ben realised how little he knew about Roman warriors. He looked strong and fit with large bare sandaled feet, big toes and thick ankle bones. Ben's gaze was fixed as the lone man moved across the floor. He wasn't marching, or carrying a weapon, but Ben knew he was a soldier.

Wide-eyed he gazed as the Roman passed under one of the stone archways then his image fragmented in the sunlight beaming through the stained glass window, like salt crystals melting into clear water.

Ben was rooted to the spot with fear, like a statue. He could only move his eyes. The stone walls of the cathedral were gradually changing, becoming scarlet red like a flow of hot molten lava yet the temperature in the cathedral remained cool. Ben was in a state of panic, absolute turmoil, he was totally disorientated and light headed.

"For goodness sake" he screamed 'can anyone else see this?"

A feminine voice gradually filled Ben's consciousness. It was Mae, she was standing next to him.

"Would you believe it, the guide directed me back here, you're stood opposite the Teaching window."
Mae shuffled around Ben, inspecting him. "Are you okay - you look really pale?"

Ben didn't answer, he just nodded and wiped his forehead, as gradually his sense of feeling returned.

A middle aged woman slowly walked towards them, she was petite and soberly dressed. As she came to stand between Ben and Mae, the guide, for that was who she was, made an expansive arm gesture pointing upward to a long stained glass window. She began to explain the history of the decorative glass in the Teaching window. The couple listened intently, Ben a touch blurred and fuzzy like the morning after the night before. His thoughts tending to wander.

".........and the top section is *Christ teaching render unto Caesar*," said the guide.

The word 'Caesar' reverberated in Ben's ears. A streak of fear jolted through his body. He could only stand and watch as Mae spoke to the guide, his mind elsewhere.

After a while, they politely said goodbye to each other. Ben tried to return a smile, but his face became contorted, more like a grimace. As Mae noticed, she grabbed Ben's forearm and maneuvered him away.

"I think we should get outside quickly, you still look dreadful Ben, what's wrong?

As Ben and Mae walked together from the enclosure of the cathedral into bright daylight, Ben breathed a long sigh of relief. "I think I need a drink."

Mae linked her arms with Ben who gradually found he could move easily, as they crossed the cobbles.

"Wasn't it wonderful to hear the sound of a choir

practicing, very atmospheric, especially with the organ."

In response, Ben mumbled again about needing to 'drink like a fish.'

Walking along arm in arm, Mae chirped like a singing bird, while Ben continued to gather his thoughts, desperately trying to make sense of what he thought he had just seen. Mae continued to talk to herself, as Ben slipped on a pair of sunglasses.

"We can look for a bar, but before that how about taking a quick look at Greestone Steps? They're just over from the main yard." Mae pointed.

"What steps?" Ben winced, behind his glasses.

"Greestone Steps, leading from Lindum Hill, it was a main roadway into Lincoln in Roman times."

"Just hold on Mae, I need a bit of peace and quiet for one minute."

Mae was surprised by his sudden outburst. He hadn't said what was wrong, and as she looked at him, all she could see was a dark anonymous shaded face. Under her intense gaze, Ben pulled away, and headed towards the nearest pub.

Mae waited for Ben in the beer garden. It was a warm sunny afternoon and the narrow streets in the Bailgate were busy with shoppers and tourists. The garden was crowded, but luckily Mae managed to claim a table, just as a couple were leaving.

Inside the pub Ben edged away from the bar, squeezing passed other customers and with drinks in hand , he made his way outside. By the time he'd joined Mae in the beer garden, he'd already drained his beer glass, and after handing her a packet of crisps, and her drink, he sat down and refilled his glass from the bottle of lager he was carrying.

After a while, Mae spoke.

"We didn't spend that long in the cathedral, perhaps we could go back to look around a bit, if you're not feeling queasy anymore?"

"I feel much better after a drink thanks and…." Ben paused, "I'd like to go back, but, not today."

Mae looked at him. The colour had returned to his face but she could sense that something was still wrong.
"Has something happened? You looked so pale earlier " she said softly, as she moved closer to him.

"I wish I knew." Ben sighed deeply, " I think I've seen something, but I can't explain what I've seen. Does that make any sense?"

"Oh yes, that makes real sense Ben. I'm really in touch with what you're saying." Then she paused for a minute and added, "I'm afraid you've lost me completely, I don't know what you mean."

Ben stood up, and held out his hand.

"Maybe we can make our way back to Castle Square which means a walk past the cathedral then make a return visit later, this evening perhaps."

Getting up from the seat, Mae adjusted the waistband of her skirt then held Ben's hand. The couple began to make their way back along the cobbled streets, Mae with a slight spring back in her step.

"In this road way there are markings where Roman columns once stood, just think, Ben, all those years ago BC and Roman soldiers were based here too, the Ninth Legion."

Ben looked down at his feet and saw stone markings as he crossed the road, Mae linked arms with him, together they walked on towards the cathedral. Now he'd had time to think about what he had seen, he knew he couldn't just dismiss it, the image had been too clear, but he didn't know how to share what he'd seen with Mae.

He began to question himself. Had he really seen a Roman? Of course, he knew he had. He recapped when he'd first seen the vision. Had anyone else in the cathedral seen it? If not, why?

Maybe, he should bury the whole episode. Close the book on it, slam the door shut. Then, as he continued to ruminate, he realised that somebody could have seen something. There was a glimmer of a chance that Mae could have seen something and not realized. She must have been walking towards him at the time. But how could he find out. He couldn't simply ask her, in a casual way, "Mae, did you see a Roman, inside the cathedral nave?"

"It's said when you walk along the side of the cathedral, as we'll be doing in a minute, the gust of wind that sweeps through you is the breath of ghosts," Mae continued. "Do you believe in ghosts?" she paused,
" I do."

Ben couldn't believe his ears, his mood brightened immediately.

"Mae, my little treasure, I have to say I do also, and I think we should go and see what else we can find, inside the cathedral."

Aghast, Mae stood still on the pavement. Then content and wrapped in each other's arms, the sightseeing couple made their way back towards the historic minster. They would decide what to do next when they reached the Minster Yard; besides there was no rush because together there was all the time in the world.

Search for a Model   by   Sharon Horne

A flurry of sketches and art work seemed to follow Don and Ed through the main art college doors. It was the end of term frenzy, of students flooding out of the inner city building, truly motivated, enthused to go out and use their artistic skills to create a work of art by the beginning of next term. There would be ample time and of course no-one was short of ideas or themes to be artistic with. Don and Ed walked towards the college car park.

"How long before you're back on the road then?"

"Tricky subject mate, could be weeks I'm in a real fix."

Gloomily Don adjusted the straps of his rucksack then crouched to release the wheel lock on a bandy looking pedal cycle that had definitely seen better days. Was it really worth securing? Feeling frustrated Don scowled at the world. Ed sat down on a low wall next to the cycle shelter putting his red and white stripe motor cycle helmet beside him, a devilish match with his red and white all in one biker's suit.

"Okay your bike's off the road for a couple of weeks, doesn't stop you riding pillion with me 'til things get sorted." Don snorted like a pig in a trough.

"Two weeks too long if you ask me, I'm grounded like a naughty school kid. I had plans to get along the coast, Anderby Creek maybe, perhaps make a start on some still life work, sand dunes with sea spray, or even a seascape. The Seal Sanctuary and Nature Reserve - they would have been great but it looks like that ideas out the window. And I'm behind finishing my work off as it is."

Ed began to think on his feet, accelerating into top gear. "I've got the answer if you're talking about places to go and do still life."

Don leaned forward, shifting his weight onto the handle bars of his pedal cycle. "I'm listening."

Ed was pleased Don was interested in his idea, at least he wanted to know more.

"If you're talking about still life I know where to

find a perfect model, one to die for. She's a beauty, I think she's your kind of girl."

"She, who are you talking about?"

"Ah, can't give too much away."

Don propped his cycle against the side of the shelter then sat next to Ed, who had a cheeky smirk across his face.

"What's your game, who's the model, come on you've said too much not to let on, who is she?"

Ed tried to look bemused. Silently both students looked out across the car park as groups of young people made their way to a nearby bus stop, chattering over events of the day and plans for the evening, while others packed away belongings, bags and art materials in the back of their own cars, joyfully speeding away to join a maze of afternoon traffic.

Don took a packet of mint chewing gum from a pocket in his denim jacket, Ed accepted a slither of gum as Don chewed on his thoughts.

" Okay where will I need to go to find this so called model, point me in the right direction."

Ed smiled as Don stood up to face him.

"As long as this isn't some kind of end of term joke."

"No I guarantee she's real, a lady with smooth curves in all the right places. I'll pick you up tomorrow about 9 o'clock. Bring plenty of paper, oh yeah and make sure your pencils are sharpened." Mischievously Ed eased his helmet over dark, short cropped hair and got up to leave. Don shouted, "You said 9 o'clock?"

Ed lifted his tinted visor, revealing dark smouldering eyes; he gave a thumbs up as he walked away to collect his motorcycle. Meanwhile Don reluctantly took hold of the handle bars of his pedal powered machine and pushed it forward, feeling conscious of looking a sorry sight. He knew his image was in tatters. Slipping into a rusty manual gear he made a quick exit from the college grounds. Who could the model be?

Next morning Don waited outside his front door watching the morning traffic flow along the main street. Over night he'd decided he had to look the part, there could well be artistic manoeuvres ahead. Dressed in his biking gear, full black leathers, boots and gloves and a silver metallic helmet with a tinted visor, Don looked the part without any doubt. As the familiar roar of a 750cc Ducati's Monster engine sounded in the distance, *Don The Rider* stepped towards the kerb, the morning sunlight adding a sparkle to the stripes of silver on the back of his all in one leather suit. As Ed pulled up on his power machine the purr of the engine was music to Don's ears. Passing vehicles gave bike and rider a wide berth. Ed switched off the engine and put his feet to the ground, he slipped off his helmet.

"Looks as if you're well set to go."

"Sure thing, I'm raring to go matey."

"You randy sod. Had any ideas about the mystery model?"

"Nah, no joy, haven't a clue. Hey it's not Mandy what's her name from Graphic Design."

"All I can say is she's got lovely knees."

Both clean shaven young men laughed aloud as they fastened their helmets. The motor cycle journey passed quickly along a busy motorway, miles were clocked up, a power surge that boosted Don and Ed. The rush of open air and acceleration in miles per hour were exhilarating. Riding pillion, leaning against Ed's broad back Don concentrated on his model, she had become Don's model. An ideal female that Don would be able to capture on paper, a work of art that would turn out to be a masterpiece. Leonardo Da Vinci's Mona Lisa would have to move to one side. Gradually as Don surfaced from his daydream he was surrounded by the pulsating, thundery sound of pistons driving engines in heavy articulated lorries, work horses of the road. Likewise fuel was pumped through the busy engines of cars and vans moving straight ahead like a colony of hungry ants. Both riders were in their element, free on the open road.

The trek north quickly notched up the miles and Don began to realise Ed's true direction. As motorway signs displayed mileage to the penny finally dropped, Don asked himself why he hadn't guessed sooner, the thought of semi naked female models in magazines perhaps. Ed pointed forward as Don's model came into view, Don tapped his friend's shoulder. There she was in her full glory, The Angel of the North, a welcoming symbol that stood in symmetrical, streamlined splendour. Her embracing outline was smooth, etched against a distant landscape, close beside a main road artery that crossed more than one border. A magnificent figure created by Richard Gormley, it was captivating. Ed signalled to turn off the motorway, eager to make an acquaintance with the new model.

In the warmth of the day Ed and Don casually strode away from the mean machine, their leather suits zipped down to their waists showing whiter than white T shirts. They carried their crash helmets tucked into their armpits, a real male statement. Both riders quietly stood in miniature at the foot of the angel, whose ridged body was towering yet slender. She signified the true grit of steel engineering. Don and Ed touched the meaning of magnificence, as had so many others, for the figure had polished toes where children and adults alike had sat for a photo shoot, to strike a pose with the perfect model, who would undoubtedly be an ideal specimen for Don's art portfolio.

Don quickly viewed the model, chose a profile then sat down on parched dry grass surrounding the statue. He took out a sketch pad and pencils from his rucksack, fired and ready to begin his masterpiece. Ed looked out, noticing different lines of vision and how the buzz of everyday life seemed far away. He bent down to speak to Don.

"Okay then, what do you think, a prize model ?"

"What's that, oh more than okay, think I'm on to a winner here."

Ed had to agree as he turned to face the statuesque angel, walking towards her to get close once more.

"Hands off she's mine," shouted Don as he looked up from his sketch pad. Ed paused then slowly turned around.

"I'm just going to look round the other side to make sure she's curvy on both sides, she could be flat like a cardboard cut out."

"Okay, you'll have to fill me in when you get back."

Don freely etched sweeping strokes onto his sketch pad. He knew Ed would wander off to ride around because his motorcycle always got the better of him. But that was okay because now Don was the presence of a fascinating model and because of that he didn't really mind about anything, not even having to be mechanically off the road. Instead he had chance to create a masterpiece that was well on the way. Don was now artistically inspired. He would find time to walk along parts of the Lincolnshire coastline when he returned home. There was plenty of scope; in fact Don had so many creative ideas there would be no stopping him, not even a motor cycle that needed fixing.

A Diary of Dates   by   Jay Michaels

Wednesday 21st April 2004

Aware of a car pulling onto the gravel drive, Charlotte waited with bated breath. The front door opened.

"Your tea's ruined again," she snapped, "this is the fourth week in a row. Why are you late? I even held back half an hour on tonight's tea, with a hope you'd be home before I dished it up. I don't know why I bother." Charlotte took a breath. Pouting, she placed her hands on her hips and glared at her partner. "Are you sure you've not got another woman?"

"Look I'm sorry," came the apologetic reply, apparently not at all surprised by the inquisition. "Pouring those water features took longer than I expected, I've got a backlog of orders."

"You think more of that place than you do of me!"

"Look, go and have a long soak, I'll clean up the kitchen. Then if you want, I'll give you a massage?"

"Huh, a small token," Charlotte retorted, before demanding a white-wine spritzer, then stomping off up stairs.

In the bathroom Charlotte was handed a cool tumbler. "I really do love you," was just heard over the gurgling water as it spurted from the bath taps.

"I know, it's just that I feel neglected. Of late you've spent almost no quality time with me. I understand how difficult it is running a business but I don't know why you don't get some extra part-time help."

"Not many people want me as a boss."

"Why not? You're a wonderful woman, with a light-hearted personality and a friendly smile. I'm sure some of the college students would appreciate some extra cash in their pockets," she paused, "Err…Jason was only asking me the other day if I could twist your arm and get him a job."

Mandy got close and draped her arms around Charlotte's shoulders. Seeing the passion smouldering in those hazel eyes, she let Charlotte drive the kiss. As their lips parted Charlotte added, "Then I'll have you all to myself a little more often." Her eyes sparkled, she grinned then licked her lips. Charlotte untied and dropped her towelling robe, revealing her petite naked body.

"You had better get in that bath you little minx," Mandy's stare scorched the delicate contours of flesh that stood enticingly before her. Teasingly, Charlotte wiggled her bum as she tested the water's temperature with her hand. A low growl slipped from Mandy's lips, "Behave or do you want my dusty sweaty body all over yours? God you are bad." Stilling and kissing the swaying cheeks, Mandy ran her hands caressingly down Charlotte's ribs and then a velvet touch up the inside of her thighs. Charlotte shivered.

"BATH NOW." Mandy demanded sternly.

Finally, Charlotte stepped seductively into the warm water and slowly lowered her body into the jasmine scented bubbles, playfully cupping her breasts. Huffing, Mandy left the bathroom.

Seconds slipped by before Charlotte called out. Casually, Mandy went back to the bathroom.

"Yes."

"That massage, does it have a time scale?"

"No, why?"

"I think you've forgotten that I'm meeting Guy down the Crown, at a quarter to nine."

"Damn, it will have to wait then." Mandy dryly answered.

Leaving Charlotte to bathe, Mandy headed for the kitchen. She slammed cupboard doors, in her search for something of interest. But the green monster inside her was doing a good job in distracting her need for food. Instead Mandy took a good slurp from the cold can of beer she had just taken from the fridge. Turning her attention to the television and then finding nothing of interest on any of the channels, inevitably caused further restlessness and frustration, it left her the only option of taking a shower. The growing reminder that Charlotte would return later that evening, bubbly, flirty and of course aroused, infuriated Mandy further. As she passed through the kitchen she slammed a couple of cupboard doors.

Thursday 22nd April 2004.

A day off from work for Charlotte was almost unheard of, because the Bank was always short staffed. So today she wanted to make it a bit special and her plan was to whisk Mandy off for a pub lunch.

It was close to midday when Charlotte entered the garden centre, and was greeted by her unsociable girlfriend.

"What do you want?" Mandy scowled.

"That's great, I came to offer you a free lunch!"

"I haven't time, seedlings need to be planted before they die."

The silence was static.

"I'm sorry," snapped Mandy, apparently reflecting on her behaviour. "I'm up to my neck in it. Can you please make us a cuppa and I'll give you a quick tour."

Charlotte disappeared into the shop, trying to hide her disappointment, although Mandy's tone spoke volumes, what was she hiding?

Returning with tea mugs in hand Charlotte tried to look interested as she was escorted through the plants and specialties that Mandy sold. Although inadvertently getting into further trouble by being captivated by her new sculptured water-features. They were of naked men, and the water had been cheekily routed through their stiff apparatus. She had claimed that one would look great in their garden and Mandy had blown a mental fuse, ranting and raving that she would have nothing so unsightly. The outburst seemed to prompt the end of Charlotte's visit, and she left in a huff, convinced she would never set foot in the garden centre ever again.

Having returned home, Charlotte turned on the television for company; the whole incident had left her feeling fed up and she was soon snoozing in the chair.

The bleeping doorbell, jarred her awake. Fuzzily, she checked the time on the video machine, 17.00 was illuminated. The buzzer went again. It can't be Mandy, she thought, she's not due home until seven. Who else would call? To put it bluntly they never got any visitors, only the post lady delivering the mail, and it was too late for that.

The shrill vibration was becoming annoying and she couldn't help feel apprehensive. Charlotte dawdled towards the front door. Maybe Mandy had finally got round to sending her flowers, she thought as she cracked open the front door. Charlotte scanned the smartly suited man in front of her. He wasn't carrying a bouquet.

"I'm sorry to disturb you; I would like to talk to you for a moment." Showing her his warrant card.

She led him through into the lounge and offered him a seat.

His broad smile warmed the ice-blue room. "I'm right in saying that you are Charlotte Watson?"

"Hmm."

"I'm D.C. Thompson."

Her eyes looked blank.

He coughed and gently tapped her hand, "Are you alright?"

"Um-mmm, sorry!"

"Do you know any of the following young men; James Fielding, Steve Johnson, Tim Smith and Daniel Dickson?"

"Well…yes…of course do," Charlotte stuttered, "I went to school with Daniel and the others I know from Uni. Why?"

"Are you sure it wasn't more than that?"

'Where is this leading?' She turned her head away and folded her arms.

'Charlotte?'

She nodded, refusing him eye contact.

"At the moment they are all apparently missing, and you…"

"What do you mean *missing*?"

"As I was saying, you seem to be the last person to be seen with them. You went out with each one of them, is that correct?"

"Yes. We went down to the pub. It was a harmless drink at the Crown." she paused, "I go out with a boy once a week, nothing exciting just a chat, like mates. Oh, but apart from James, I had a game of pool with him. Meet up with him once a month, not due to meet him again until a week on Wednesday. It's always the first Wednesday of the month. That will be the 5th of May."

"Do you keep a diary?" he queried.

"I'll go and get it. Err, just one thing!"

"What?"

"Daniel was my first boyfriend; we were an item at school and we're still reasonably close. Although we have on occasions been driven to… you know?"

"In your words, please."

"Oh God, this is embarrassing. Don't write this down. It has to be off the record. We take precautions, safe sex and all that. Mandy would kill me if I got pregnant. The thing is Mandy and I well; we're a couple okay? And she doesn't know, that Daniel and I can't quite finish it."

"Let's see if I got all of that, Mandy is a Lesbian, then you must be bi-sexual?"

"Yes, if we have to label it. Nobody knows that we're a couple. *She*, sorry, told me to keep the male dates to one a week as a cover. She was frightened that if the truth got out, the business would lose money though being boycotted."

"I get all that, so for the moment I will keep it to myself but if it becomes relevant to the investigation then I'll have to release the information." He paused, "Diary?"

Charlotte jogged upstairs and back.

"A quick question, now that you're back. Were any of the four young men in a state of depression?"

"No."

"It's all right I understand how difficult this must be. Can you give me the dates of your nights out for the last two months?"

"Okay, today is 22nd April 2004. That would take us back to March.

Wednesday 3rd March, James Fielding.
Wednesday 10th March, Daniel.
Wednesday 17th March, Daniel.
Wednesday 24th March, I saw Steve Johnson.
Wednesday 31st March, I saw Tim Smith.
Wednesday 7th April, I saw James Fielding.
Monday   12th April I met Daniel for lunch.
Wednesday 14th April, Daniel.
Wednesday 21st April, last night, I saw Guy, first date."

"Have you by any chance seen or heard from any of them since your date?"

"No…" she whispered.

"Where do you work?" he enquired.

"A Bank, Lloyds –TSB, I've had today off."

"Do you own the house?"

"I wish. No it's Mandy's. She also owns the garden centre just down the road."

"Does she know any of the young men?"

"Not that I know of, they may have gone to buy plants but I don't think so. They weren't into gardening, and she wouldn't know their names, but I suppose there is no harm in asking her. She won't be home until 7ish tonight and she'll be at work 10 am -5 pm tomorrow, so you could catch her then."

"Does she have a mobile phone?"

"No, just the work's phone."

"Have you any plans for next week…on Wednesday night?"

"I'm meeting Nigel the decorator's son, I don't know his surname."

"You've been a great help Charlotte, thanks, I'll see myself out."

Charlotte felt numb and what's more, she desperately wanted something alcoholic. She scribbled a note to Mandy, grabbed her handbag and left.

The Crown pub had just opened its doors for evening trade. Charlotte ordered double vodka with lemonade, and was scanning for a quiet seat when somebody tapped her shoulder. Turning, Charlotte's face lit up at seeing the friendly face.

"I've been calling you, but you didn't seem to hear. Are you all right? You look terrible."

"Thanks Matt, that's just what I wanted to know...Give us a hug, please."

"There is a seat over by me. Come and tell me your woes."

After a swift mouthful of drink, Charlotte enlightened Matt with the details.

"Do you think Mandy has anything to do with this?"

"God knows, although she's been working extra hours and spending less quality time with me. I hope in a way she is jealous, then she'll come home earlier. I have to come clean. Mandy is the one who pushed me to go out on male dates. She was trying to divert speculative gossip about us. Mandy thinks the villagers still have a mentality of the dark ages and she's scared that they will boycott the garden centre." A lone tear trickled down her cheek and Matt leaned over and wiped it away.

"Look we've been mates for years, let me take you to dinner and cheer you up, there's no strings, just good company. What do you say?"

"Why not, next Friday night okay with you?"

"Great, I've got a little Italian in mind I'll pick you up at 7.30pm."

They carried on talking for another hour before Matt walked her home.

Friday 30th April 2004.

They were tucked in the corner, with pasta, garlic, and red wine. The meal had been magnificent and she listened attentively as Matt talked about work. It delighted her to know how much he was enjoying working as an investigative reporter, for the neighbouring county newspaper. And what surprised her more was that she was drooling over him, even though she had eaten sufficiently. Charlotte was drowning in the depths of his tropical-coffee eyes, and yearned to be wrapped in those protective natural dark-skinned arms. He had kept his slender proportions, not skinny, strong but not over muscular. Being petite, she normally went out with men of similar stature.

"Charlotte, I've really enjoyed tonight, thanks for the company. What did you tell Mandy?"

"That I had a staff meeting, then we were nipping to the pub for last orders."

"Was she okay with that?"

"She didn't query it. Why the interest?"

"I don't want to create a row between you two, that's all. Um… how did your date go with Nigel?"

"This is strange. I'm not used to having someone interested in my dates, but just so you know, I will not be going out again with either Guy or Nigel."

"Why?"

"Well let's just say, it wasn't fun, as the date is just a chat and a laugh, nothing else. I really struggled to get them to talk."

"Great, that's what I hoped to hear, no competition. So I can freely ask you out again, that is if you want to. Monday night in The Crown for a drink, I can meet you at eight?"

"You're on." Her pupils widened, her heart pounded, and butterflies fluttered in her stomach.

"I had better take you home." Matt moved closer for a kiss but decided against it. He was content to have her seated beside him on the drive home.

Monday 3rd May 2004.

In the Crown Matt was seated at a table. He was quietly sipping his pint of Lager-shandy, and worried at Charlotte's lateness. She had spoken to him on Sunday on his mobile and hadn't cancelled their date. Another twenty minutes passed, then Charlotte rushed in, crimson and shaking. She sat down beside him.

"Are you all right?"

"I think so… I've had a row with Mandy, she's being stand offish and won't tell me why."

"Does she know you're meeting me?"

"No… and she has no reason to suspect anything. She refuses to come into this pub, she'll only go to the Black Horse in the next village."

"Let me get you a drink."

"Smirnoff Ice, either red or black but in a glass please…thanks." she said, moving out of his way.

"Is the pub normally this quiet?"

"What do you expect for a Monday? Matt you should try it on a Wednesday night. Why don't you come and join me again? If you survive tonight."

"What do you mean?" he queried.

"Sorry, I didn't mean to imply that anything, would happen." Her eyes watered. "Oh God, as you've brought the subject up, the bad news is Guy and Nigel are officially missing."

Matt watched her cautiously, tears slipped down her pale cheeks. Charlotte shook her head.

"What's going on? Why is this happening? I don't understand." Looking straight at Matt, blinking, she wiped the salty wetness from her face with the back of her hand.

He offered her a crisp white hanky, and held his tongue for the moment.

"Who would want to hurt them?"

"Are they hurt?" he asked.

"How should I know?" she retorted. "*You*, you think I had something to do with their…" but she was unable to finish the sentence. People were staring at them.

"I wasn't insinuating anything, it's just that six men have gone missing, no suicide notes. Apparently no instability, no personal phone calls or ransom demands. What do you think happened to them?" Matt whispered.

Charlotte's whole body shook.

"Let me take you home." he placed his coat around her arms.

"No! I'm sorry…I don't want to see Mandy yet. Can we go for a walk please? Its not too cold outside."

"Sure. I'm sorry too, but I thought you should know about them." He said softly and placed his arm around her shoulder.

They walked towards the park, and ended up sitting on the swings, talking. At eleven thirty, Matt escorted her home.

"Can I meet you Wednesday for dinner or a drink?" he enquired.

"Perhaps, but what if you're next?" Her tone was full of fear.

"I'm a big boy," he smiled, "you are more important to me. Take care. Ring me, Charlotte, at home or on my mobile, it's no problem."

She nodded, leaving him on the path in front of the house.

The next few days dragged by, Charlotte had to occupy herself as Mandy was in a foul mood and keeping her distance. Opting to spend more time at the garden centre, saying she had things to do. Apparently she had plants that need to be prepared, ready for the horticultural show at the weekend.

Charlotte enjoyed the Wednesday night date with Matt. He was really great company, thoughtful and sensitive, making her laugh and relax, which made a change from Mandy. Coffee was set up for the Thursday lunch, so she could see that he was alive and well. They made plans for Saturday night to see a film.

Friday 5th May 2004

At the garden centre Mandy was using her mobile. The part-time staff member was due in at eleven, which gave her a few minutes to ring Matt. The spacious glasshouse was designed as a shop and the small side-room for tea making facility or for consuming lunch. The fridge had to go somewhere cool.

Mandy kicked the cupboard then swore at the pain.

"Is everything ok, boss?", asked the cashier.

"Err, what? Have you been there long?"

"No, sorry, just this second walked in. Why?"

"Nothing's going right today, one of the deliveries is late, I was chasing it up."

"Kettle's warm if you want to do the honours; I'll just go and open the gates for business."

Mandy muttered under her breath at the closeness. Matt wasn't going to be as easy as the others. They had all visited the garden centre without a quibble. Guy delivered information for hotels and restaurants that she wanted to surprise Charlotte with. Nigel, the decorators' son delivered colour charts before he went camping. Daniel, James and Steve all wanted some extra cash so they did some deliveries for her and jobs around the garden centre. Tim strangely wanted to take her out for a drink, happy for some girly company.

It was amazing how useful that forklift truck had been, unloading peat, sand, and supporting the unconscious. Even that class in model making had come in useful. Learning to make a shell that encases and contains liquids and substances after decay. Covering this with cement gave the shape more ruggedness and authenticity, as if chiselled from stone.

Monday 8th May 2004

At the police station, Matt was waiting in one of the interview rooms for D.C. Thompson.

"What do you want Matt?"

"Huh great, nice way to treat an old friend."

"I've got nothing to say at this point, on anything."

"No messing, I'll get straight to the point, *the missing boys*."

"Can't comment."

"Tom, this is serious. I'm here to share information with you, not the other way round."

"What?"

"I've been entertaining Charlotte Watson, we go way back, dinner dates and drinks. All under cover, anyway, I know you've reached a dead-end."

"So how can you help?"

"Here's Mandy's mobile number."

"Damn! I was told she didn't have one."

"Well it's assigned to the garden centre. When she's out, if the staff have a problem, then they just ring her."

"Great, how come you…?"

"Mandy rang me on Friday and tried to arrange for me to meet her for a drink. Luckily I was in Manchester covering a story. I spoke to Charlotte last night and when I asked if she had mentioned my name to Mandy, she almost bit my head off."

"I'll get the number checked out immediately, see if she made calls to any of the missing men. If her number comes up then we'll get her in for questioning. Keep me posted if you find anything else out?"

"Will do."

"Thanks for this, makes a change you giving me info. Be careful Matt."

"I intend to."

Tuesday 9th May 2004.

At ten thirty in the morning, Matt suspiciously eyed the name highlighted on the face of his vibrating mobile before answering it. Mandy was extremely excited, she begged for him to come and meet Charlotte, as she was waiting for him. She said Charlotte couldn't talk to him as she had just rushed to the Ladies. Slightly troubled he rang Charlotte's mobile. It was turned off. Next, he tried her at home and got no answer. He still felt wary and phoned the Bank for some kind of verbal confirmation. Cautious, Matt spoke to D.C. Thompson as he left the office building.

It took Matt ten minutes to drive to the garden centre, drawing the car to a stop beside the huge gates. A metal chain with the word CLOSED dangled loosely through the iron bars. His hand rested on the gate. For a second he was worried that it was a trap from which he wouldn't escape, then his concern for Charlotte out weighed his unease. Heart pounding, Matt alertly entered the yard and scanned for the unusual. The shop door was ajar.

Keeping his eyes peeled, he pushed it open, the hairs on the back of his neck standing out.

"Thank God," squealed a female.

Matt jumped, startling by Mandy's appearance, which had seemingly emerged out of thin air.

"I was starting to panic. I've sprained my wrist and can't drive. You need to look at Charlotte. She's slurring words and rambling."

Matt's gaze scanned Charlotte's pale dusty face. There was a cut above the right eye, a tiny trickle of blood, it was trying to clot, purple-blue coloured the area. '

"First aid kit!" yelled Matt.

Mandy fetched it.

"What happened?"

"I don't know, just found her like it. We'll have to wait until she can tell us what happened."

He felt Charlotte's forehead before cleaning the wound. It was hot. Talking to her, he could see she was dazed, as she was slow to answer and couldn't recollect what had happened. Matt lifted her eyelids to see how her pupils reacted to the light. It pained him to see Charlotte hurt.

"Ah," she moaned, when he dressed the wound. The sweat was running down Matt's back, he mopped his brow. Mandy held out a glass of orange juice. For a moment he stared at it, he couldn't make out if the sun was heating the room or the heating was on full blast. His dry tongue stuck to the roof of his mouth, so he drank.

"She should go to hospital, Mandy," he said when he had finished his drink.

"Why what's the diagnosis?"

"Not that I'm a doctor, but probably concussion, or maybe a fractured skull. Where's the telephone?' he said searching his pockets and feeling slightly stupid that he'd left his mobile in the car.

"Uh in the office… that big shed in front of you!" Mandy stammered, clinging to the counter for support. "Is she going to be all right?"

"Well I've seen worse. Do you want a chair?"

She pointed to the back of the shop. If this was a set up then Mandy was a great actress, he thought when he'd returned with the seat.

"You sit, I'll be back in a mo."

Mandy watched Matt sway across to the shed, using the door for support, he shook his head. Leaving Charlotte, who was practically unconscious, Mandy went to his aid.

"What have you done?"

"Nothing yet, you've just had a little drink of orange juice, oh with added Rohypnol. It will relax and then put you to sleep."

Matt stared at her.

"Surely you've heard of that."

"Of course," said Matt, " it's the date rape drug."

"So," continued Mandy, "in about another ten minutes you'll be unconscious and I can inject you with Curare. A plant poison, that will kill you."

"Why?"

"I don't want to share Charlotte with anyone."

"But you suggested it, a cover so that you wouldn't lose customers if they found out you're a lesbian."

"So she told you that did she! Well I didn't give her permission to sleep with them!" snapped Mandy.

"Who told you?"

"Jason, her so-called friend, because he was jealous and furious that she had turned him down. He blabbed."

"But she never slept with any of them."

"Oh so what are you, her fairy godmother? You're the last of her boyfriends."

"No, we're friends, mates I've known her for years."

Mandy laughed, "Yes, and I'm a genie."

"What have you done with them?", Matt managed, knowing it was about the last of his questions as the poison was taking a firm hold.

Mandy pointed, to the sculptures stood to the left of her. " That's Guy and Nigel, the others I've sold. Now you can see what you'll become? Something useful, and deliver a flow of water for-ever.' She chuckled. "It's a shame that there's not a sustainable body market for me to use. I've enjoyed hiding the evidence."

Matt slumped to the dusty floor, slipping into unconsciousness.

Grinning smugly, Mandy removed the bandage from her wrist and headed back to Charlotte. She was please to find her still seated and dazed. *That blow to her head worked a treat,* she thought, *that would teach her not to speak to me in that tone.* Mandy leaned into the fridge for the plant mixture, and took it back to the shed and her unwanted guest. Reaching across the bench, Mandy grabbed a pair of surgical gloves, pulled them on and carefully filled the syringe with the deadly liquid. Bending down beside Matt's limp body she hunched forwards, stabbing his chest with the sharp needle, and energetically forced down the plunger, empting the contents into his lifeless body.

"Police, don't move, put your hands in the air! "

The shout came from behind her. Startled, Mandy froze.

"Stand up slowly! You're under arrest."

D.C. Thompson applied pressure to Matt's carotid artery in his neck. He felt the regular pulse… as it faded, he engaged in mouth-to-mouth.

"You must watch the next bit, it's fascinating. Oh, a lovely shade of blue, it's respiratory failure you know." Mandy gloated.

"What's Charlotte going to think?"

"That you're a bitch, and Matt didn't deserve to die, come to think about it neither did the others. You think I want you after this. You're mad. I hope they throw away the key." Charlotte snarled clinging to the shed door.

"I love you…"

"Don't." scowled Charlotte.

"Dan, take her away and get me the medical examiner." demanded the officer.

The Mirror   by   Lisa Spinner

Donna had an estate auction to attend today, her client had passed on and had left an enormous amount of wealth behind, but with no family to leave it to, it was going to be split up and auctioned off to the highest bidder. Donna went from room to room in the grand house making sure there were enough chairs for prospective buyers, that the auctioneer had a glass and jug of water and all the usual bits were running smoothly.

On her way back to her desk she visited an old mirror that she had had her eye on. It was about 6ft tall and as wide as a doorway. It was framed in dark mahogany with decorative eagles and flowers carved into it. At the top stood a lonely wolf carved beneath a passage. It read: - *reflections in speculum es non verus. Peto devia unus, vel defluo eternitas.* Donna had the passage translated as it intrigued her, it read: - 'Reflections in the mirror are not true. Seek out the lonely one, or be lost forever'. She had fallen in love with it from that moment. Although she knew she could never own it, it was well out of her price range even with all the commission she could make from this job it still wouldn't be enough. She admired it once more and then left. The phone on her desk was ringing; she went to answer it. "Parker's auctions, Donna speaking".

"Hi Donna its me. What time do you think you'll be home?"

"Why?" Donna asked.

"Well, I was gonna cook; you know candles, soft music…"

"You're to good to me Steve. Should be about 6ish"

"Ok then, don't work to hard, love you," said Steve.

"Love you too, oh wait a minute can you pick up my grey jacket from the dry cleaners? I don't think I'll have time," said Donna. "No problem" said Steve.

Donna heard a noise in the auction room and went to investigate. She found nothing out of the ordinary. She turned to leave and the mirror shimmered. She wasn't sure what she thought she saw. It shimmered again, as though it was trying to get her attention. Donna ran out of the room. "Did anyone else see that?" She looked around she was completely alone. Helping herself to a glass of water from the auctioneer's table she tried to calm herself down. "You're just over tired Donna that's all, the mirror didn't do anything, they can't do anything they're just inanimate objects" she said to herself.

She heard the noise again. Donna peered round the corner: she didn't know what to expect but the mirror seemed normal. She gathered her strength and decided to approach the mirror. Standing in front if it Donna eyed it curiously; walking round it she looked for something to explain what had happened, she found nothing.
Had it been her imagination or had the mirror shimmered; as she turned to go it did it again. "I thought so," Donna said to her reflection. Then was when it happened.

"Help me" the reflection spoke. Donna was quite startled. She took a couple of steps back in surprise. She was sure she hadn't spoken.

"Help me". No it was the reflection. Not sure if she was cracking up, she wondered if the pressure of work was getting to her. But she was still curious. "How?" Donna asked. "Place your hands on the mirror touching mine, I'll do the rest". Donna hesitated a moment. She looked around to make sure no one was watching then placed her hands on the mirror. It was unusually cold; a tingling sensation filled her body. The air crackled; her ears popped, Donna closed her eyes. A feeling of being dragged through an icy blast of wind chilled her to the bone. Then it was calm, her temperature returned to normal and she opened her eyes. She came face to face with her reflection; except this time Donna could touch her - she was real.

Spinning round to see the mirror behind her and the room she had left, but no reflection of her. The mirror shimmered again and the glass splintered into a thousand tiny pieces that fell to the floor. Uneasy, Donna asked her reflection "How am I going to get back?" Unemotionally her reflection said, "There's no going back, you're here forever ". "No, that's not possible I have a life" Donna said not wanting to believe her reflection. "So did I once, we're all stuck here" said her reflection casually as she walked away.

The Courier   by   Lisa Spinner

The piercing sound of the alarm clock broke the morning silence. Errrh, murmured Alan as he reached for the snooze button. He rolled over and muttered something about 10 more minutes. His subconscious was already up, dressed and downstairs having breakfast but convincing himself to join it was a little harder. Half an hour later saw him downstairs packing his bag for work. "Is it Wednesday today?" Alan asked.

"Yes it is. Why what's the matter?"

"Oh nothing, gotta go or I'll be late," Alan said as he was finishing a slice of toast on the way out of the door.

"Bye" he said over his shoulder to Ellie his wife of 9 years as he was walking up the drive. He Reached his car when she caught his attention from the sitting room window

"Darling don't forget your sandwiches, here catch" she threw a small red Tupperware box towards her husband.

"Have a nice day".

"Thanks love" he replied as he caught the box and drove off to work.

Alan was in his middle forties, 5'8" and had a figure that had been well cared for especially in the alcohol department. He'd worked as a courier for a large logistics company for just a little longer than he had been married. He used to hate Wednesdays because they were always the busiest day of the week. But now with the new guy who had started he found himself enjoying them again. It made them into a slower paced day these days. Alan retrieved his paperwork from the office and went off to find his van. It had taken him an hour to plan out his route because it varied from day to day. He packed his white van carefully so he could find each parcel without too much trouble. With a bit of luck he would get to see that lovely Alsatian that lived at No.64 Sunnyvale close. Alan had always loved dogs, but his parents wouldn't let him have one as a pet when he was younger.

Outside the weather was pleasant enough at the moment although it looked like it might rain later. He preferred travelling on the back roads between villages because there was hardly any traffic. On the way to his first village Alan had to slow down as he came up behind some traffic. "Come on you can go faster than that!" Alan said as if the person in front would be able to hear him. "The speed limit is 40 round here you know; I'm sure a Volvo can do that". The needle on Alan's speedometer was just touching 30. Alan hated slow drivers. He wished they would pull over and let the people who actually had places to be and things to do get past.

Soon enough he reached the crossroads "Thank god he's not going my way" said Alan as he indicated right. Two minutes later he was in the village of Tinby where the Alsatian he liked lived. He looked at his manifest sheet "Damn…no parcels for them today, never mind I'll see them some other time". He did a couple of other deliveries here and he was back on the road.

Alan sped along the back country roads. Coming up to a T-junction Alan eased off the speed to let the car up ahead turn on to the road and build up speed. It was a blue Volvo. Slowing down even more behind it he recognised the license plates. "Oh no not you again" Alan drove behind him patiently. After a mile he could feel the irritation smouldering under the surface. "For god's sake" Alan could see that the man driving could barely see over the wheel. The reflection in the rear view mirror showed he wore thick black-rimmed glasses, had grey hair and looked quite elderly. *Obviously out for a Sunday drive* he thought and doesn't care who he holds up. "Oh, Oh nearly reached 35mph then, you'd better slow down your speeding way too much" Alan had had enough he couldn't take it any more. He beeped his horn and flashed his lights but it made no difference the Volvo continued to crawl along at its own pace. With anger and adrenaline bubbling to the surface and seeing a clear stretch of road ahead, he indicated, floored the van and sped past shouting "Where did you get your licence a cornflake packet?" Bloody drivers shouldn't be allowed on the road if they can't keep up with the speed of the traffic. Alan glanced at the clock in the van; its bright green display showed 4.15pm he'd wasted about 10 mins being stuck behind him. Time was difficult to keep up with when he had a lot of deliveries. He just about had time to do three more drops before heading back. After one wrong address, and a rather anxious guard dog barking like there's no tomorrow, he delivered his final parcel. Typical no one in, it nearly always happened sometime during his route. He filled in a leaflet to inform the owner when and where they could collect their parcel from and posted it through the shiny brass letterbox.

Back in the van Alan looked at the clock again: it was 4.45pm. If he made good time he could get back in time to see his father when he arrived. His father often visited them just to prove he was still capable of doing things by himself. Only 5 miles or so to go, I'll take the back road so I don't get caught in the road works and rush hour traffic he thought. Speeding around the corner he had to brake sharply; there was a line of traffic in front of him. It was probably a tractor and trailer or a herd of sheep possibly. Slowly the traffic overtook the slow moving vehicle. *It's not possible* he thought; the slow vehicle was the little Volvo meandering along at 35pmh again. Thank god his turning was just round the corner.

Eventually back at the depot he parked his van, finished his paperwork and drove home. Removing his key from the front door he heard "Hi darling" Ellie called from the kitchen where she was making him a coffee. "How was your day?"

"It was a bloody nightmare," he said as he hung his coat up. "I got stuck behind this Volvo that couldn't do more than 35mph. I'm sure it was an old man that couldn't see above the steering wheel" Alan sat himself in his comfy chair, "He drove like it anyway. People like that shouldn't be on the roads they're a menace," he said. "Never mind love you're home now, just try and relax here's your coffee. Dinner will be around 7.00pm ok. Oh I think your father's just pulled up. You stay there darling I'll go let him in".

"Thanks sweetie" said Alan enjoying his well earned coffee. Alan's father entered the sitting room looking rather flustered. "Hi dad, how's your day been, did you manage to get the plants you wanted?"

"Let me sit down first son, Ellie how's about one of your special cups of tea?"

"Ok I won't be a moment" Ellie disappeared in to the kitchen.

"Cheers love" said George.

George lived with Lillian his wife of 40 years in a little bungalow a few miles from Alan's house. He was in his late 60's. He wore thick black glasses and was always wearing a cardigan to match his shirt. He removed his brown flat cap, which had been moulded into position by time and constant use, revealing his grey hair neatly combed and framing his experienced and well lived-in face. "Oh son what a day I've had."

"Here's your tea George," said Ellie as she handed him a slim white cup and saucer. "Let me tell you it started when I went to collect those plants I've been after. I had this white van man behind me most of the day. Impatience and downright rudeness is what I call it. He was flashing his lights and beeping his horn and once sped past like he was taking part in a grand prix or something. Its not like I could go any faster. Some people have no manners at all on they road, do they?"

SCM Ghosthunters Ltd by   Mavis Wilkinson

The curtains were drawn. The word curtains is a gross exaggeration. Two grey tattered fragments of lace hung dejectedly joined together as ever busy spiders spun their webs.

Sarah was standing on a metal upturned bucket we'd discovered in the dilapidated greenhouse and trying to undo the sash window. She knew it would open, she'd explored this manorial hall many times over the years it had stood empty and neglected. She'd found secret passages, hidden doors, heard spooky noises and actually seen ghosts or ghoulies as she always called them in her teenage tomboy manner. She feared nothing!

Now, I was helping to break into this grey stone mansion which nestled majestically at the foot of the Lincolnshire Ridge. Sarah, my ex best friend had invited myself and her new best friend Christine to join her in a spot of ghost hunting. I'd made excuses. I'd got to help my Dad empty the toilet, the Beatles were going to be on the telly and as a last resort, I needed to write my Henry VIII essay for Monday's history lesson.

"What's the matter", Sarah asked, "are you scared of being caught by the ghoulies? You've got to come. The new people are moving in soon and we'll not be able to nose round then. Anyway, all good things come in threes, three wise men, three Musketeers, the three ghost hunters that's us, SCM Ghost Hunters Ltd .

I was tempted to add three little pigs and three blind mice and why was her initial first and mine last in our company's title. I can't remember ever accepting her invitation but somehow Sarah had persuaded me and so here I was on a sunny Sunday morning, climbing over the ancient and unbelievably cold stone windowsill into a small chilly room.

I was terrified. I was now a criminal. My parents would punish me severely if they found out what I was up to and scariest of all, I was probably going to meet a ghost.

"I think this was the larder" said Sarah in a posh voice mimicking a tour guide.

I think she was right. Wooden shelves lined the distempered walls above a huge stone slab. I followed my fellow directors into the vast kitchen.

" Come on Maz. The ghoulies will catch up with you if you're that slow. This is the kitchen, once used to provide meals for the visit of Henry VIII. Put that in your essay."

It was common knowledge that Henry VIII had visited the hall and its inhabitants who had been well regarded in royal circles, but this kitchen held no clue to that event. At the far end was a grease encrusted Aga and midway down one side was a white sink standing on brick pillars. That was it.

Suddenly. there was a fluttering noise and with my heart pounding, I squealed a silent scream and shot behind the door.

The two so called friends laughed. "It's a bird you daft idiot. There's a hole in the window pane. We knew you'd be a laugh."

Was this why I was here? To be the stooge.

Sarah passed me, giving me a condescending pat on my shaking shoulder. We climbed the huge wooden staircase. I'd planned to place myself in a safe place between the two comedians, but Christine had Sarah's dress belt firmly in her grip. Reaching the top, we were guided into a large room darkened by the wood panelling which lined the room from the decorated ceiling to the oak floor.

The leaded windows shone enough of the day's sunlight so I could see a stone fireplace sandwiched by two wide doors.

Sarah positioned herself for her next tourist announcement. " This is the bedroom where Lady Standworthy died." As if on cue, footsteps could be heard through one of the doors. They got louder and louder as I shivered with fear. Somehow my lead lined jelly legs ran down the staircase and through the larder window.

Funnily enough, I could see the ever brave Sarah way ahead of me. We ran through the wood and into the village.

"Sorry about that" said an obviously petrified Sarah, " needed the toilet urgently." She ran into her house followed by Christine who slammed the door shut. I think that was the moment that SCM Ghost hunters Ltd disbanded.

Still shaking I ran home passing the church yard where Lady Standworthy's grave peered over the wall. Mum was pleased to see me as the beef joint was ready. Unusually I wasn't hungry and made an excuse that Sarah had insisted that I test some of her own baked Eccles cakes. I spent the afternoon trying to concentrate on my Henry VIII essay but Ann Boleyn's beheading was nothing compared to my horrifying experience. Sleep didn't come easily that night, and when it did, a gigantic piece of wood panelling was walking towards me with a bloody head nailed to it.

I arrived at school the next morning to hear Sarah bragging to the class that she'd been talking to Lady Standworthy's ghoulie, and that I'd been a nervous scaredy cat all day. I realised that I was glad I was now Sarah's ex best friend and decided I'd try to put the whole incident to a back corner of my brain.

That was until Tuesday teatime. My father spoke " I was talking to Ken down the village this morning. There's been a break-in at the old hall. The new people went in on Sunday afternoon and discovered the crime. Think it happened Sunday morning. You were down the village Marilyn, did you see anyone about?"

Weak legs again. My face turned bright red, partly because of guilty embarrassment, but mostly because my potted meat sandwich was sticking firmly in my throat. I should have worn gloves, the police will be fingerprinting everyone. My mother thumped my back and retrieved my soggy food.

"Was anything stolen?" she asked

"Yes, a bathroom suite and some plumbing stuff."

Things suddenly became very clear. I wasn't sure whether to be pleased or not. Which would have been worse: Lady Standworthy's ghost in the bedroom with the wood panelling or the burglars in the hall with the copper piping. I think my answer was best, run like hell through the larder with the open window.

The Top Prize   by   Mavis Wilkinson

"1965"

"No, 1966."

"It was definitely 1965. Our family went to Bournemouth. We called at Bladon and saw his grave."

"Winston Churchill's my relation. I should know when he died."

"What relation?"

"My husband had a cousin whose husband's aunty married the second cousin of a member of the Churchill family."

"Practically your brother then."

"Winston's my hero. He won us the war. Victory was Winston's."

Kate relented. She never agreed with Lavinia and her opinions. Jim, the landlord of the Red Lion demanded their answer sheet, so Joan scribbled 1965 and handed it in. They were one of ten finalists in the New Year Pub Quiz.

Their team, the Monson Lane Residents consisted of four contrasting women.

Lavinia, from the Hall. In her seventies, her white hair styled in a soft bun. Clothed in a classic dress with a claret cashmere wrap warming her shoulders, her specialised subjects were opera, music, horses, wine and French cuisine. Lavinia knew all the answers and jolly well said so.

Joan, retired to a rose adorned stone cottage. Brown brogues, tweed skirt, pink twin set with three strands of pearls. Her strengths were literature, musicals, gardening and travel. A thoughtful respected lady.

Annie, fifty, existed in a dilapidated caravan. Attired in her hippy dress, bedecked in cheap beads, her long greying locks held tight by a headband covered in charity badges. She spoke in whispered grunts unless the subjects of nature, animal rights or politics came up.

Kate, forty seven, lived in a council house and wore her uniform of jeans and a Lincoln Imps shirt. Vital for sport, entertainment, television and her passion, history.

Jim the host continued, "and the last answer in the What's the Date round is 1965. Churchill died in 1965."

"Told you." sneered Kate.

"All right" said a disgruntled Lavinia "But the victory was Winston's again."

Joan interrupted. "We got all ten right. We've only dropped three points in four rounds. We could win"

We have to win thought Kate. I need the top prize. John, her husband had been ill for months and the doctors had diagnosed a rare type of terminal cancer. They'd experienced the shock, upset, anger and despair and were now determined to enjoy their time together. It had been John's ambition to produce a book on Lincolnshire Churches. Their children bought him a digital camera and they had explored hundreds of churches from All Saints, Pilham, a tiny building to the grander St Lawrence's at Bardney with its Abbey stones . The ancient St Edith's at Coates to the plastic coated St John the Divine at Southrey. She had to win the prize of a computer, donated by a local business man as a friendly advertising gesture. John could write his book. It was vital she won.

"Right," said Jim, "natural world. What is a smew?"
Annie shuffled. "Bird, duck like, Russian."

They soon had eight more points, then another ten as Lavinia bulldozed her way through the culinary round.

"The last round, and we have two teams on level pegging."

One must be us, thought Kate, it's got to be. The Tennis Club team cheered confidently as did the Yeller Bellies.

History round and between the four players they were confident they had nine answers right.

"The last question of the night. Who wrote A History of the English Speaking Peoples."?

Kate smiled "Winston Churchill".

"No." shouted Lavinia. "They wouldn't have Winston twice in one quiz."

"I think it could be a modern writer, perhaps a David Frost report."

Kate insisted. "I don't know if it's reports, a novel or what, but I dust it every week on our bookshelf."

"Well, we'll put that," said a wise Joan handing in their last quiz paper.

Break time and jacket potato, meat pie and peas.

Lavinia had potato. "Not really my cuisine."

Joan had a potato and peas. "Pie's stodgy."

Annie ate potato and peas. " Never touch murdered animals."

Kate tucked in to a plateful of everything. "Great, a decent meal."

"Right." said Jim. "Results time. In third place, the South Lincs Fishers."

Cheers and jeers all round as Gemma the barmaid handed them third prize, a box each of snowman shaped shortbread.

"Second place, the Yeller Bellies." Each contestant was handed a box of chocolates depicting a robin on a pillar box.

"First place, decided on the last question." The Tennis club shuffled ready to receive their prizes. Kate just prayed. "And it's the lovely ladies from Monson Lane."

They each received a bottle of red wine.

Lavinia spoke, "You were right with Winston then. This claret will go nicely with my supper." Joan put her bottle on the raffle. Annie mumbled something about marrow stew and Kate smiled politely and thought she could put it on her chips.

Now was Kate's chance to win that computer for her beloved John. The team were up against each other.

"The subject for this final is Lincolnshire."

Kate was relieved. She stood a chance.

"No help please. Ladies write down your answers and Gemma will collect them in. Number one, Where was Alfred Tennyson born?"

The four women frantically scribbled.

" Who lived in Woolsthorpe Manor ?"

Kate's grandparents were buried in Colsterworth just round the corner from the manor.

"Three. Which Lincolnshire village did George Stubbs dissect horses in the name of art?"

Yes! Kate knew this. She'd taken her friend to Horkstow looking for ancestors and heard the story. The others didn't seem to know the answer.

"Number four. John Harrison invented the marine chronometer. Where did he live?"
Oh no, Kate knew this was either Barrow or Barton on Humber, but always mixed up the two.

"Right the results. Somersby. Well done all of you. Isaac Newton, three knew this. Horkstow, only one of you got that, and Barrow upon Humber.

Kate was mortified. Barrow you idiot not Barton.

"Well it's between Lavinia and Kate. First person to shout out the right answer wins this lovely computer. Who's statue can be found in the town of Spilsbury?" Kate shouted, "John Franklin!"

She was in a daze as everyone clapped and cheered. She'd won the computer. John could write his book. Tears flowed.Lavinia was the first to congratulate her. "Well Lavinia," cried Kate, "I've got to agree with you on one thing. The victory was Winston's after all."

Bad Satellite Rising   by   Rachel Gardner

The curtains were drawn, and three lights were set on time switches: she was only planning to be away for one night, but some of Martin's habits were hard to shake off. She deliberately refrained from going back to check that she'd locked the front door.

"*Move away from the vehicle*" her car said as she approached it. Startled, Dawn thumbed the remote again.

"*Move away from the vehicle.*" The cold, metallic tones sounded like Martin at his most aggrieved. Just don't let the alarm go off. The car repeated "*Move away …*" and fell silent as she turned the key.

"Now, where are we going?" Dawn said out loud, fiddling with the gearstick lock Martin had insisted she used every time she parked. The steel hoop popped out with a sulky little clunk, and she turned her attention to the GPS navigation system, her pride, joy and extra brain.

"Mm, North Kyme, North Kyme…ah, North Kyme, Lincolnshire, got you!"

The sun was already sinking as she pulled out of the drive, lighting up the mellowing bricks of the garden wall, and Dawn smiled almost tenderly, remembering how Martin had fussed over them. Even during his last spring, it had been "Dawn, have you done the garden wall recently?" until there had been nothing for it but to fill the black bucket with hot water and Jeyes Fluid and scrub away every shameful trace of green or grey. The moss and lichen were coming back for good, now: the wall was finally starting to look real.

"*At the end of the road, turn right,*" said the car, calm and sober as the voice of the Shipping Forecast. "*Continue for 300 yards.*"

Dawn changed up, squinted into the sun, and flipped a CD into the stereo.

"At the next junction, go straight ahead."

Johnny had made her the CD, a jumble of songs that had been playing in all the pubs they'd ever met in, touching warm fingers wrapped around cold pints. Bootleg music, illegal downloads, Martin would go spare. Out on the High Street, she hummed along, checking the fuel gauge, watching for pedestrians, waiting for her next instruction.

"At the roundabout, take the second exit."

Johnny lived out in the Fens, where the ground was like a serving dish with a dome of polished steel sky clapped over it. Dawn had been to his house twice before, but he'd been driving; all she had seen had been a ribbon of landscape unrolling on either side of his black-leathered shoulders. She couldn't navigate to save her life, not even sitting in a quiet passenger seat with a map on the dashboard. When Martin had been in a good mood, he'd teased her about her sense of direction.

"He only hit me once" she said out loud, startling herself with her own voice.

"Continue for four point five miles" said the car as they left the Bracebridge speed limit and the A15 unrolled. Dawn turned up the volume on the stereo. The creeper covering Johnny's house would be bright red now – in the first frost, the path would be ankle-deep in autumn, and the house windows would appear like the pictures in an Advent calendar. Maybe they'd sweep the leaves up this year; maybe they wouldn't.

"At the next junction, turn left."

Maybe she'd plant crocuses on Martin's grave – it was still the right time of year. Silky purple crocuses like an empress's French knickers, and eggy yellow ones that the sparrows would tear up; big flaring goblets of crocuses that would keep the sexton from mowing the grass there till May.

A car coming out of Billinghay flashed her, and Dawn realised it was getting dark. Guiltily obedient, she switched her lights on.

"Why can't you do that for yourself, car?"

"At the next junction, turn left."

"Are we nearly there yet?"

She thought she must be: this road was narrow, the white line as faded as a scar, trees cut back to tractor height. The headlights picked out the hanging broken branch too late: it scraped thin dry fingers down her paintwork, and the aerial hummed like a tuning fork.

"At the next junction, turn right."

Left and right led to identical darkness, the black weight of a massive embankment straight ahead cutting out the orange glow of street lights in the distance; road-dirt and algae were obliterating a once-white signpost.

"Tattershall Bridge, hold on… we don't want a bridge, do we? I'm sure we never crossed the Witham before – but then, this does look like the Witham…"

"At the next junction, turn right" the car repeated. It didn't usually repeat itself, and it was starting to sound impatient. Dawn glanced in the rear-view mirror, saw no approaching headlights – nobody would get impatient and start hooting while she dithered – and peered at the signpost again.

"Turn right."

Her foot was on the accelerator and her hand on the gear stick before the meaning of the words had arrived in her brain – she took the corner without indicating, gasping "I'm sorry, I'm sorry!" The dull chimes of a fifth-generation Charlotte Green clone had suddenly acquired the bitten tightness of a man speaking without moving his lips. The road wound, and the black bank paced it like a dog; there were houses one after the other, she was taking this bend too fast, but there were lights ahead…

"At the next junction, go straight ahead."

It was a big junction, she was going too fast, there was nothing coming, street lights and over, back into darkness. That had been a main road, hadn't it, she'd seen Coningsby on a signpost, but that was some little part of her mind talking to itself, clicking its abacus while the house burned down.

"Christ, I hate driving in the dark" Dawn said under her breath, unlocking her hands on the slick plastic wheel. The orange glow dwindled behind her, and the car filled with clicking and ticking, heralding the resonant opening chords of Pink Floyd's 'Welcome to the Machine'. Hold on, this track had been on once already: had she been driving that long?

Dawn didn't even see the next junction. *"At the first opportunity, make a U-turn"* said the car, still in that tone of tight-bitten patience, and she stopped dead, reflexively hitting the hazard switch. Orange bushes came and went outside the windows. The road was scarcely wider than the car, with a drain on either side. She couldn't turn, she couldn't reverse, she didn't know where she was, that voice was going to speak to her again if she didn't do what it wanted, and she *couldn't*… Dawn pulled herself together as she'd done so many times before, fought back the tears of panic, glanced at the fuel gauge and drove on. There was a hissing rustle as she picked up speed, a dry moth-wing fluttering in the dashboard: the air intakes were sucking in dead leaves, blowing withered brown confetti out of the vents.

"Make. A. U-turn."

It was plainly a man's voice now, clipped and restrained – a man riding the tiger of his anger with a tight, tight rein. She snapped the stereo off, feeling the music fraying the strands of her attention, and saw the farm gate just in time, barely enough space to turn in. She crept the back wheels into the track, did a five-point reverse-round-a-corner, but the voice said only *"At the next junction, turn right."*

This wasn't right: the roads were getting smaller and smaller. North Kyme was on a main road, the A something-or-other. She'd been driving for an hour and a half...a 30mph speed limit sign! Street lights, a name, civilisation! She could phone Johnny, get him to come and find her, it didn't matter how much he'd laugh. When Johnny was here, her dead husband wouldn't talk out of the car dashboard to her, everything would be normal, nothing could stay frightening when Johnny was there to laugh at it.

The mobile in the glove compartment gave one sullen beep and shut down, battery dead. This was not going to daunt her, she was efficient: the car charger was in the glove compartment too, along with the breakdown cover documents and a clean pair of...what was that? The busy silence of the open line, in the gap between dialling and ringing, was filled by the hard, dry fluttering of dead leaves in an air vent. She pushed the connector more firmly into the dashboard. There was no ringing tone, but she heard the click: the phone had been picked up.

"Johnny, it's me, Dawn, I'm so sorry, I'm going through this place called Chapel Hill, but I don't know which way because I don't know how I got here –
the GPS isn't working and I can't find you..."

"Carry on straight ahead" Martin's voice said in her ear.

"Johnny, this isn't funny, it's dark and I'm frightened and I haven't got much more petrol…"

"Carry. On. Driving."

Dawn yanked the phone connector out of the dashboard, swerving wildly across the road on a bend which fortunately – suddenly – flared wide enough for an oncoming car to miss her with room to spare. Maybe this was the right road after all, maybe Martin was looking after her. The road was straight: she could put her foot down, do sixty, though it rose and fell like a fairground ride. Fenland subsidence: everything sank eventually, squeezed in the flower press of the peat. Martin always had looked after her, he'd only ever wanted the best for her.

"At the next junction, turn right."

It was still Martin's voice, but calm and confident now, and the junction was a real one, with a gleaming modern signpost, a crash barrier on the bend, and a scatter of houses beyond. Moments later, she hit the first pothole, saw the road crumbling at the edges, sagging into the drains, ending in darkness – no, turning through ninety degrees, a bend even Johnny's bike couldn't have taken. The car went into a wild skid, the screech of tarmac under the locked tyres giving way to a roar of gravel, and even as Dawn thought "Thank God, there's a track there, not a drain" it plunged like a wrecking ball into the corner of the derelict farmhouse beyond.

The dog walker who was first on the scene begged the Fire Brigade to hurry, swearing that there was someone still alive in there, under the collapsing bricks and the flames, but when the man's shouts and the woman's screams gave way to stern lecturing and penitent sobs, he guessed it could only be a radio, somehow still playing in the wreckage, and tried to think no more about it.